I TAKE YOU

Also by Nikki Gemmell

I TAKE YOU

A NOVEL

Nikki Gemmell

HARPER ● PERENNIAL

NEW YORK ● LONDON ● TORONTO ● SYDNEY ● NEW DELHI ● AUCKLAND

HARPER ● PERENNIAL

First published in 2013 in the United Kingdom by Fourth Estate, an imprint of HarperCollins Publishers.

P.S.™ is a trademark of HarperCollins Publishers.

HarperCollins books may be purchased for educational, business, or sales promotional use. For information please e-mail the Special Markets Department at SPsales@harpercollins.com.

First Harper Perennial edition published 2014.

Illustrations by Jo Walker

Library of Congress Cataloging-in-Publication Data has been applied for.

ISBN 978–0–06–227341–3

14 15 16 17 18 RRD 10 9 8 7 6 5 4 3 2 1

I TAKE YOU

1

Each has her past shut in her like the leaves of a book known to her by heart, and her friends can only read the title

Four a.m. The prowling hour. The wakefulness comes into Connie like a blade flicked open, for ours is essentially a fearful age and she is a child of it. All her choices in adult life have been dictated by fear and now, in the early hours, it curdles.

Fear of entrapment. Of being found out. Of turning into one of those women for whom indecision has become a vocation, of a silent slipping into that. Of emotional sledging, that she is becoming less resilient, not more, as she sails beyond youth. Of softening into fat, of men who take note as if she's ripe for a mugging, of life settling like concrete around her and judgement; of what people think of her, yes, that most of all. Women! How awful they can be.

When does the unliving start? For a particular female of this particular age, it is incremental. For Connie – ensconced in her five-storey villa in London's Notting Hill that was once splashed creamily across the pages of *Architectural Digest* – it has begun.

2

The eyes of others our prisons;
their thoughts our cages

But there is one small pocket of Connie's life where there is no fear.

Quite the opposite, in fact.

None of the people in her regular world of kick-boxing with her private trainer in Kensington Gardens, of ladies lunching around the communal table at Ottolenghi and of shop scouring, endlessly, on West-bourne Grove, knows of this place. In this one tiny corner of her existence all the blushing is left behind; she is unbound. Connie blooms in this world, into someone else entirely. It is a place that is open with possibility, with the potency of power, and she has so little of that in her regular life. It bequeaths her little moments of vividness that have become like scooping a hand into cool, clear creek water in summer's heat.

3

Blame it or praise it, there is no denying the wild horse in us

Cliff has called. He has asked Connie to be ready in two hours. He is taking this late afternoon off – rare in the silky world of a Mayfair hedge fund manager – and a car will pick her up. Her stomach rolls in anticipation, as he speaks, it rolls as if a steamroller is gently travelling over it. The tugging, deep in her belly, the wet; at the whispered command, it has been a long time, too long, since this.

'Prepare yourself.'

Connie waits for the car on the Lockheed chaise longue – made entirely of riveted aluminium – by its tall window in a mewly winter light. She loves how the metal of her coveted design piece looks like a giant goblet of mercury, like something else entirely; thrills at the sternness of it against her flesh. Its arresting cold. She is shaved, perfumed; this is all necessary now. To her, and to Cliff, dear Cliff, to whom she has been married for four years and with him for five before it.

Connie is dressed well. Always, she is dressed well. A woman who has the instinctive touch of looking impeccably 'right', on every occasion; conservative, with a flick of cool. Today, it is the shortened Chanel skirt of grey bouclé with veins of red through it. The iron-grey, silk Chloé blouse that slips like water from Connie's hands and hangs below the jacket cuffs with something of the loucheness of the seventies to it; a touch of Bianca Jagger in her prime. The black lace Rigby and Peller bra, fitted by the Queen's fitters. Wolford stockings. No knickers. Shoes, vintage McQueen's, that look like the snout of a bull terrier. Fearsome, hobbling, but Connie has mastered them; everything in her rarefied life appears gilded, effortless.

She must be entirely shaved, of course. 'I need you bare,' Cliff has whispered, his voice dropping an octave as Connie squeezes her thighs together, tight, so tight, upon the thought. Bare for whom? What?

The car, sleek and panther black, purrs to a stop outside their villa which backs onto one of Notting Hill's finest communal gardens, an expanse of several hidden acres now silent with snow on this January afternoon. A pristine, waiting brittleness. It has been a particularly long winter. One pair of footprints, heavy workman's boots, smear the glary expanse of the great lawn like the restless prowl of a lone wolf; but no child plays, no adult wanders. The sky is pale, almost white. Everything waits. But for what . . .?

The lady of the house picks her way carefully down the icy marble steps. She smiles her too wide, too unEnglish smile at Lara Deniston-Dickson, her neighbour, who is nudging recalcitrant window boxes into spring preparation after winter's clench; checking on the wilted cyclamens that withstand so much. Lara is one of the few Brits left on this square. Her dilapidated house is crammed with fabulous but shabby heirlooms, oak dressers and chairs, a dining table piled with books, washstands, a zebra rug, ancestral portraits, a Modigliani from Granny, several pianos and a lot of dust – the servants have long gone, as has the heat. It is one of the few houses left like this on the square as the bankers have sharked in, mainly from foreign countries, everyone, it seems, but the Russians because this is still not Belgravia, still a bit too ragged, edgy, loose for that lot. Lara has a grand disdain for this new world that has gone into lockdown, barricading the riff-raff out. Even her husband, dear Rupert, a man of some standing, thank you very much, yet treated like a tramp, asked by the new committee if he 'owned' – if he deserved a key to this very garden – merely because he was old and a touch scruffy with it. Oh yes, Lara has a disdain for these shiny, refulgent newcomers with their babies in cashmere and men in their too-new Barbour coats, all of them; except for the poor, lost girl next door with her dazzle of a smile that illuminates her face as if she is lit from within, but she doesn't see it enough.

She does now. 'Going out?' The older woman smiles in approval, for she likes to see her sweet slip of a neighbour getting some fresh air, cheeks flushed; bound as she is to her workaholic husband and his precise demands. Connie knows little of his previous life, she has told Lara that.

'I have no idea where,' Connie laughs. 'Do you? No, I didn't think so. It's a complete surprise. He adores them. To a quite ridiculous extent.' She is talking of her husband as if he is a little boy.

'He's a keeper, that one.' Lara nods, smiling, a woman who has lived through three marriages and four children. 'A good marriage is fed with kindness, of course, but surprise, the gift of it – now *that* is the hidden ingredient. To sparkle things up now and then. Absolutely necessary in my book.'

'Oh yes.' Connie waves a pale hand nonchalantly, a hand manicured three times a week, upon which sits a single ruby within a protective ring of diamonds that once encircled the finger of Wallis Simpson. 'Oh yes,' she repeats, stepping into the warmth of the idling car and staring into her husband's eyes as he waits in the back seat, spinning in the deft fingers of his left hand his Mont Blanc Bohème Noir pen. The pen that has been everywhere, that has begun all this; with the words it wrote, with the secret world it sprang into life.

4

She had the perpetual sense, as she watched the taxicabs, of being out, out, far out to sea and alone; she always had the feeling that it was very, very dangerous to live even one day

The car pulls seamlessly away from the kerb. The windows are smoked to blankness. No one can see inside. Connie sits upright, legs delicately crossed at ankles, the worn crocodile of her vintage Mulberry handbag demure on her lap. She does not look at Cliff, she never looks at him, at the start, she can't, she will stumble if she does. The spell cannot be broken; she must not let her head intrude, her rational thoughts; it is the only way these tumblings into something else can work. These episodes when she lets her body's anima, the dark recesses of her mind, take over; when she trusts, completely trusts, because he has unlocked her into this.

The car is driven through the jangly upper reaches of Ladbroke Grove – as opposed to the White Heights, what Cliff and Connie call their rarefied end of Notting Hill in a private joke – and takes a left at the end of it. Their cars never take a left. Connie still does not look at Cliff, she neither asks nor questions. She gazes out the window as she is transported further and further from the graciousness of her home, her tree-lined street. A new London entirely unpeels before her.

A very different London – the real London, possibly – skinned before her eyes. A world of unremitting ugliness, scruffiness; not a blade of green in sight. The great press of its people, from all walks of life; everywhere but Britain, Connie thinks. It feels like these poor, watchful people are the stranded backwash, left high and dry upon a cowed, groaning, exhausted plot of earth. Connie's from Cornwall, where the earth still sings, the great, beautiful bones of an ancient land and when she catches scenes like this it feels like the joyless future of this island, of the world; the crowded, jostling, built-over and unhappy future of the world as they know it. Feels like her tiny, lovely little Kensington and Chelsea is ring-fenced by the crushing, resentful, triumphant press of . . . this. The utter lack of any attempt at graciousness and wit and reach in this new England is startling, jarring, wrong; yet Connie feels like the only person in the world so thoroughly disturbed by it. These people need beauty too! Nowhere, here, is the London of her imagination that she moved into to gulp aged twenty-two.

Fingers suddenly spider across Connie's soft inner thigh. It is the whisper of an enquiry, tracing a finery, her names perhaps; to submit, to begin. It is the signal. She turns from the window. Obediently, beyond will, beyond thought, Connie unhooks her legs and parts them, just a touch. Sits upright, very still. Waits. The fingers gently, gently nudge up her skirt until it is bunched in a thick band around her waist. She is ready, as directed, with just a plain black suspender belt. No ribbon, no lace, the thrilling cold of the limousine's leather seat pressing up onto her, into her. The driver's eyes flick at hers. She catches them. It is a new driver. She holds his gaze, her face gives nothing away; he is trying not to look, he looks down, at her bareness splayed on the leather, he cannot help himself. Cliff's fingers softly, gently, part her lips, as if for the driver's benefit then circle, exploratory, her back passage then suddenly plunge in – she gasps, lurches forward – then his fingers find her other hole until she is hooked and now poised, exposed, on the crook of his hand as her own reaches down, unstoppably, as she spreads herself, unstoppably and exposes her clit wide and presses her forefinger down on it and moans. She shuts her eyes on the driver's glance, on the greyness of the world outside, on the weighed-down people at their drab little bus stop and the Halal chicken shop and another right beside it as she grinds down unstoppably on the cool leather of the seat.

'I want to inspect you,' her husband whispers. 'You have to be fully prepared. Nothing must be left to chance. Remove your skirt.'

Connie obediently slides down the zipper and wriggles out of it. Loops the shirt ends up into the top of her bra, for maximum visibility, holds her hands obediently, waiting, across her breasts.

The driver's eyes. Cliff and her need others, now, need to elaborate; need to shift away relentlessly from sameness.

'Come,' her husband commands.

Connie climbs across the wide interior to her husband's seat.

'Sit.'

She straddles her husband, her back to the driver; she goes to kiss Cliff but veers to the left of his cheek at the last moment and hooks her chin on his shoulder. He lifts her body high. 'Yes,' he whispers, examining her cunt with his fat pen, parting her lips then running his fingers in luxurious strokes along the wetness then lifting up her hips so that her behind is fully exposed, high, so high, to the driver, and Cliff is parting her cheeks wide, wider now and she is like a baboon there, poised, with her ready arse. 'Display yourself,' Cliff whispers and she parts her cheeks with her own hands, flattening her belly and moaning and pushing out her cunt, as wide as she can for the driver, for her husband, for any camera that may be filming for she is now, entirely, someone else. Poised. For the next step, whatever it may be.

'Your Maglite,' her husband says to the driver in another voice entirely.

'Sir?'

'Please.'

The driver fumbles in the glove compartment to his left and hands a tiny, slim torch across. Cliff switches it on and runs the beam across Connie's wideness then he turns the torch around, switches it off, and toys the blunt end at her anal opening. The shock of the cold, the thrill of it. She groans, starts to move under its questioning, the chill pushing soft against her resisting bud. Cliff works it and works it until Connie is tightening her muscles and coming in a spasm of wet and collapsing against his strong shoulder that's like a sudden scaffold to her limpness.

'Yes. She's ready,' Cliff smiles. 'Proceed.'

'Yes, sir.'

The car revs yet does not lurch, never lurches, all is smooth and seamless and utterly correct.

5

*The world wavered and quivered and threatened
to burst into flames*

How far will you go? When do you stop? Have you stopped, have you shut down, did you ever start? Bow out, now, if you must. When is the spell broken so that the inhibition, the flinching, the admonition and retort come rushing back? Have you put this down yet? Once, Connie would have thought a woman could have died of shame but instead of which, the shame died. Just like that, so D. H. Lawrence wrote. Shame, which is fear. And judgement. And with the death of shame she was released. A regular, everyday woman, any woman, of demure and considered tastes; raised by an empowered mother to be an empowered woman and yet deep down she was plumed into transcendent life by this. How? Why? It doesn't make sense, yet it seems like something deeply animal, biological, these moments of vividness when she surrenders to something quite disconnected from everything else in her life; baubles of otherness, oh yes. Surrenders her body, by relinquishing her mind, such a delicate balancing act. And so Connie is released, for nights like this, to become someone else. Entranced. On the cusp of an unimaginable fate . . .

The city peels away, the car drives on, out into open country and through villages bunkered down against the cold and they're gone in a flash and then they're bulleting along runnels of narrow, high-hedged green and then thick woods, on, on, through the waiting quiet. The snow-scrubbed day has absorbed all sound.

The car suddenly, smoothly, pulls over into a small clearing. Without a word from either man. As if this has been done before. As if all is proceeding to plan. As if they are in some kind of strange, unspoken collusion. Connie jerks up her head, like a dog suddenly alert; lights are in front of them, but at a distance, high, wide; something momentous is close. She has no idea what. She trusts.

'For his little task I need you to lie across my lap, my lovely, but up, up, on all fours,' Cliff requests politely.

When Connie is done, arranged, as to specification, he whispers to her, 'Do you love me?' a moth's breath to her ear, the pen in his hand stroking her labia, the familiar pen.

'Yes, yes.'

Something is reached for, it is hard and cold, it suddenly penetrates her anus, is switched on, it buzzes. 'Yes, yes,' she repeats as she flinches, groans, widens herself.

'Will you do what I want? Are you my good girl?'

'Yes, yes,' as the car pulls away, soft, with barely a murmur and certainly no signal, no talk.

The gatehouse they come to, a short distance away, is a frippery of sculpted sandstone three storeys high. The car slows through its high arch and stops. Connie is on all fours, still, naked now except for her stockings and McQueen's; her haunches across Cliff's lap, her willing cunt exposed high to the side window which the driver now lowers. A shock of winter cold, a crunch of gravel, a low West Country voice commanding a flurry of dogs to 'git, the lot of you, be still'. Torchlight sweeps the car. Connie does not turn, does not look, stays still, pliant, tremulous, waiting, entranced; anonymous, as she knows she should, as she knows she must. For it is what Cliff wants. She is the good wife.

'We're here for the doctor,' Cliff says, the V of his fingers spreading her as if in some secret prearranged signal. 'We're ready.'

'But is the lass?' a man says with a rough laugh. The heat of a torch, suddenly close upon Connie's cunt. Examining, considering. Fingers, gnarled, rough, brusque, brushing aside Cliff, roughly spreading her lips. Connie does not turn, does not look, she gasps at the shock, folds into it; signalling her need, her readiness, her want.

'She's been prepared. She's wide enough where she needs to be.' Cliff kisses her cheek lightly. 'And narrow enough' – another kiss – 'where she needs to be.'

'Off you go then. They're all waiting.'

Connie's rump is smartly slapped like a mare set off into pasture.

6

The truth is, I often like women. I like their unconventionality. I like their completeness. I like their anonymity

Snow is raggedy and undisciplined, in big, blowsy flakes as Connie steps from the car. Naked but for her stockings and shoes, naked against the visceral shock of the cold. Cliff is already out, thanks to the driver, he is readied, silken and immaculate, by her door. The driver now removes an ankle-length mink coat from the car boot and wraps it around her and hooks it, just once, at her neck; the silk of its lining cool and comforting against her skin. Her face is blank, as is his. 'Thank you,' she murmurs and as he finishes adjusting the fur at her shoulders he brushes his hand, once, swift, along her wetness in its entirety and up her belly which rises softly, subtly, to meet his cupped touch. 'Thank you,' she repeats.

Face blank, he turns to Cliff who is patiently waiting, smiling and holding out his hand for Connie; the two of them like the crème de la crème of a society ball about to glide into their grand moment; as if all is precisely as it should be. Connie crunches through snow as resistant as a frozen grape. Tugs the coat shut against the snow, the chill, the opened door ahead of them and its spilling light but Cliff shakes his head – 'uh-uh' – it is not what he wants and so she steps inside that beautiful, warmly lit Jacobean building, through its wall of heat, with the coat ever so slightly open and fluid to her readied, strummed nakedness.

Before them, a high desk. Of the kind found in an exclusive nightclub. A lone woman is at its helm. Slicked-down blonde bob, scarlet lips, bustier; Vivienne Westwood, Connie guesses.

'Good evening.' Cliff nods, ever the gentleman.

The woman looks at Connie. Takes a riding crop from the desk before her and inches the fur coat open with it, as if to assess. A wry smile, one side up one side down. Approval. The woman rises from her desk, and it is then that Connie and Cliff realize she is wearing nothing but that bustier, her pudenda a strip of blonde, her cleft strong and visible underneath. She walks right up to Connie, thrusts a hand between her legs. 'Is she ready?' she asks, moving closer, cunt to cunt. Connie can feel it, the shock of another woman so violently close, her energy, her challenge; she flinches and reels back, has never been with a woman before, doesn't know what to do. The receptionist draws back and gazes at her, with what? Fondness, pity, wonder. What is ahead, what . . .?

'I'll let the master of the house know.'

They are all in collusion, Cliff is in on it. Part of the excitement is surrendering completely to his control but the two of them have never gone this far before. A prickling of discomfort; Connie quells it. The element of surprise, of teaching unfolding, has always been a crucial component of this journey; like being blindly led further and further down a secret path. Where will it end? How? Connie is astounded at her trusting capacity to shut off mentally in order to transport herself physically; her deep willingness for the drug of transcendence. The desire to go deeper and deeper down that secret path, whatever is at the end of it.

The receptionist makes a call – 'She's here, the main act, you promised me a go' – then explains to Connie her face will be covered so she is truly anonymous, and free, that she has to be as free as she can be tonight or it will not work, it can't, she has to surrender completely or it will not be any good . . . 'for me, for you, for any of us' . . . but then they are interrupted by a man of fifty or so bouncing down the imposing wooden staircase and warmly greeting Cliff with a shake of both hands.

'Welcome, welcome, my friend. Ahmed is waiting. And this – *this* – must be the beautiful Constance.' The man unhooks her coat and throws it back from her shoulders. 'Can I watch?' he asks Cliff, never taking his eyes from Connie, the length of her waiting, ready, primed body, utterly exposed to the three of them. 'It would please me immensely. It's been a long time since we had one of these.'

'Be my guest.' Cliff nods in the smoothly charming way he has with his clients as he extracts their money from them.

'And everyone else?'

'But of course.'

'Excellent. The theatre, the good doctor, the instruments. All are ready and waiting, my friend.'

A suddenly violent flinch, flaring through Connie, like a horse's shudder. Cliff takes her hand – 'I love you so much' – he is whispering his approval, his gratitude, steadying her. 'The next step. For both of us. Your gift to me. To us.'

Connie is righted, almost buckles, with anticipation,

readiness, want. Nothing must break the spell, nothing, she must not rationalize too much. She must not let fear clench her want, dissolve it.

'*Surrender – completely – or it will not work. For me . . . for you . . . for any of us.*'

7

For most of history, anonymous was a woman

A young woman is summoned, her hair in a plain bun. She is bearing a silver tray. The receptionist picks up a length of silk cloth and wraps it several times, with practised expertise, around Connie's eyes and cheeks, her belly firm into her back. 'My name is Nika,' she whispers. 'And I'm going to look after you tonight.'

The master of the house observes, takes over. 'The cloth is so no one knows who you are in the real world,' he explains, 'so no one will ever know. Tonight, our little club is packed. They are being thrown morsels as we speak but you . . . you . . . are what they want. They have been told something of what to expect. And none of them will ever know who you are. Or who you belong to.' Cliff squeezes her hand as the master reties Nika's knot tighter and whispers in her ear. 'Anonymity is your refuge. Your liberation. Into another world, another life. You are one of us now. You will be ours from this night. You will want to be.'

He steps in front of Connie and parts the silk, just a sliver, so she can see out, for now, a touch. His fingertip brushes down her lips, he smiles, their secret.

'Nika, please escort my old friend into the red room. He needs some pre-show entertainment. And perhaps a stiff drink. I need to prepare this dear girl.'

At that, Connie starts trembling; trembling as she

realizes this is all entirely new, and Cliff will not be with her, not leading her, telling her what to do, not whispering a kiss on the cheek and assuring her everything will be all right; she is trembling as the maid takes her husband by the hand and leads him out, away, from her, from whatever is next; trembling as she realizes she is now alone with this man with his sudden greed of a touch. For what, she does not know. Have they gone too far, Cliff and her, in spilling their secret wants? She never expected that world to leach into real life.

It is too late, Cliff is gone.

The stranger throws her fur coat briskly on the counter. 'We'll be needing none of this now.' Summons another girl from the shadow of a doorway, also bearing a silver tray. Upon it is a thick red collar. 'Such a pretty little thing, for a pretty little girl,' he murmurs, buckling it around Connie's neck then suddenly tugging it roughly, pulling it a notch too tight as if he is free, now, to be vicious, since his friends have left the room, like a man in a secret moment with a dog. The collar is too thick, the leathery smell pungent. Connie gasps but does not cry out. 'Oh, you sweet, sweet thing, you are ready, so ready for this, aren't you?' A chain is attached and she is jerked towards a wooden door, low, with brass studs. Roughly pushed through it. She stumbles. A foot in the small of her back forces her up, into looking.

A room like Connie has never seen before. Like some anatomical theatre of old. Small and windowless and steeped with hard wooden benches on three sides, on several levels. In the centre of the floor: a narrow, unforgiving doctor's table. Instinctively Connie knows it will be hard and cold upon her flesh, for it is for her, instinctively she knows that. It has steel railings at its head, like a bedhead, for securing things she presumes, and stirrups hanging down from the ceiling above. Next to it is a narrow steel table with various implements; she can hardly bear to look, she is breathing fast now, shallow; there are irons and manacles, collars, whips of different sizes and some strange instrument that looks like a medieval hole-puncher. How has her world come to this? Where is Cliff? No, no, she must veer back into willingness.

'Yes, my dear, oh yes,' the master murmurs, propelling her towards the table, grasping her chin and forcing her into looking. She pulls back, resists, the man immediately calls out 'Hans' and through the door steps a man in tight jeans and singlet, no neck, just a fall of skin into shoulders and with two panting dogs on leashes; all three of them look like they've been plucked from the London just driven through. He has her fur coat over his arm. One dog barks. Connie is very, very still, scarcely breathing now, trembling.

'Just remember, my love, this is what Cliff wants,' the master says, mock-soothing, holding her leash tight so they are now cheek to cheek. 'He has asked for this. For everything. He will be in the audience. He needs to know how much you love him. How obedient you will be. For him. For others. It's what he wants.' Connie whimpers. 'You know that.'

She does. Everything she has done beforehand has led to this point. She shuts her eyes, wilts. Her tongue is nailed to the floor of her mouth. The master takes her mink from his servant and spreads it upon the doctor's table, fur side up. Connie knows, now, what she must do, what is expected of her. She does not resist, it is what Cliff wants, it is what she wants, what she has led him to think she wants. She steps obediently up onto the small platform by the table. Slips off her shoes and places them carefully, side by side, on the floor. Lies down gingerly, for she knows this is what Cliff has prescribed; in his precise way, he has thought this through carefully. She says nothing as the bouncer secures her wrists with iron manacles and ties them to the iron bars at her head. Surrenders, gasps. Says nothing as he trusses her up, knees bent, violently exposed, for the entire theatre to see; says nothing as the bouncer runs a finger across her, slips a digit in, grunts his approval. A dog barks, comes forward, Connie moans. The servant withdraws, too quick. Is gone.

And now. Just the master and her. He walks around the theatrical space in a circle, assessing. 'We certainly don't need these,' he says suddenly, crisply, taking out a small ivory penknife and running it down the Wolford silk on each leg, snapping off the garters. Expertly, no skin is broken. Connie cannot see, can barely move, she is so bound. A tongue laps her up, once, quick. Her arse is rimmed, entered. A groan.

So ready, so ready.

'I'll leave you for now,' the master says, looping the dogs' leashes over a post by the lowest seats. Then he kisses Connie gently on the forehead, caresses her like a child being put to bed. Adjusts a surgical light so it is glaring onto her and steps away. 'Enjoy. You are extremely lucky to have someone who allows you to be so utterly, magnificently . . . free.'

He is gone.

*   *   *

Connie hears the door shut, the panting of the dogs, the faint hum of the light. So. Utterly alone. Anonymous. Another person entirely. And waiting, wet. Within the valley of her mind; her roaring raging glittering mind. All the shaded creek pockets like crypts; the beauty and ugliness, the rawness and the want. The night feels open with possibility. How ironic this is, Connie thinks; how ironic that like so many suicides these actions can stem from nothing more than a simple desire to be good. It is the obedient, the pliant, who succumb, who always succumb. The selfish, the craven, the canny – those with the chip of ice – would never get to this point.

Yet the enthralling power of it, too. The thrilling sense of command, of being watched.

Wet, so wet, as she waits, like a spring-loaded trap ready to lock its jaws upon life. Anonymously. Entirely someone else.

8

Lock up your libraries if you like, but there is no gate, no lock, no bolt you can set upon the freedom of my mind

Connie can barely see through her sliver of silk. The banked seats are full. The animal anticipation. Cliff there somewhere, anonymous, hidden, but she can't make him out. She is exposed, in the glary light, yet no one can discern who she is. She waits. A gong, a frisson of silence. Backs straightened, straining. A ringmaster strides in. He cracks his long whip either side of her and she gasps and flinches at the shock but is untouched. The audience cheer. Then the stirrups begin to move, mechanically, straightening her legs, forcing them apart in a violent V. The audience, primed, thunder their approval.

'This act, my friends, this last act of the evening, is called . . . The Banker's Wife.' A roar of approval. 'And to assist, we welcome to the floor a physician who deals with the most unusual, most delicious, most singular of situations – the esteemed Dr Ahmed. Normally, these requests are carried out in utmost privacy. But tonight you are extremely fortunate, for what you are about to witness is to be shared, by consent, with all of you.' Roaring, stamping. 'Now, is she good and ready, I wonder? Is she the banker's wife – or the banker's whore?' He is working the crowd, revving them up. 'Does she want this, I wonder? Let's see, shall we?' Clapping, cheering, whistling, jeering. 'I can't hear you. Shall we see, or shall we not?' Roaring, and at that moment Connie realizes that they perceive it all as artifice, pretence, she is part of a theatrical show, one of many put on here, it is all an act, she can play a part. She surrenders; her body a receptacle for whatever Cliff has decided upon next.

The ringmaster holds out his whip, suddenly smiles, thinks twice, turns it around, and with great show of a drum roll nudges the handle inside Connie's vagina. She'll show him, draws it in, knows Cliff is watching somewhere close, aroused, his face unmoved yet profoundly moved and she writhes on that handle, grasping it in her muscles and working it, rhythmically working it, for she knows he wants her with others, always asks; other men, women, in a place like this; more than anything he wants this, he has told her often and she comes in a flood, the good wife, too quick, in her own private moment amid the spectacle of the crowd, his gift to her and hers to him.

As she collapses inward, with the sheer exquisiteness, a small man of great containment, neatness, steps from the shadows. The crowd hushes, expectant.

The next step.

'Good evening. What you are about to witness tonight is a most unusual – but not uncommon – request.' A naked woman steps forward, wearing nothing but a red collar with a chain looped from it, firm under her cunt, from front to back. She is holding a red velvet cushion upon which sit three small devices. The man picks up a tiny object, displays it high. 'What you see before you is a padlock. Not quite the usual one. It has a nicely rounded shape. It is has been made by artisans, to the husband's exact specifications.' A glittery quiet. 'Quite a beautiful little treasure, oh yes. A ruby surrounded by diamonds is embedded on one side' – the audience gasp – 'and a swirl that echoes an esteemed family crest is engraved upon the other.' He snatches it away. 'Ah! No peeking!' The audience laugh in excitement. 'It is a most singular and exhilarating form of marital binding.' He strokes the underside of Connie's thighs, she shivers.

'The subject is ready and willing. For her husband. Tonight. We will be inserting two sleepers in a most intimate place; these will be the rings that will hold our pretty padlock in place. From this moment this sweet, willing, and very good wife will feel its presence at all times, reminding her constantly of her most rarefied role. Thrilling her, stimulating her, disciplining her. Whenever she sees another man she wants, she will bear down on this secret bauble, knowing it is her husband and her husband only who has the key. And yes, he will allow others, at times, at his choosing; perhaps, even, if we are so lucky, within the hallowed walls of this club. Others will be allowed to touch this . . . open it . . . bestow the thrilling gift of release. Have your way. You see, this is a man of decidedly singular and specific wants. And his wife is extremely beautiful – and wanton – and greedy.' His finger circles Connie's anus. Cacophonous laughter. 'Now, where exactly is this charming little object to be placed? I wonder . . .'

His fingers brush across Connie's bared and readied labia, she gasps, writhes, glancing at the menacing hole-puncher on the steel table. Of course. Dr Ahmed picks it up. The stirrups move again, forcing her into the first position that she was left in for seeming hours, forcing her still, utterly bared. Her eyes search the audience for Cliff . . . he must be in the shadows . . . somewhere near a door . . . discreet as always . . . knows it is what he wants . . . has requested . . . the logical step . . .

'You will not wear underpants after tonight,' he had whispered in the car, 'for me, for my associates, for all of us.' Now she knows why. 'Do you love me, do you?'

'Yes,' she is murmuring now, 'yes, yes.'

Because everything has been building to this moment, of course, this moment of the attaching of a coldly explosive little object that is to become part of her from now on, her flesh, her very existence, as much as a scar is, a pacemaker, a metal pin. Every time Connie thinks of it, its weight, its grate, its drag and its coolness, she will be reminded, thrilled, addled, snared; she will shut her eyes upon it and squeeze tight. His, his alone. Totally submissive to him. Unlocked only by him, for others of his choosing, whenever he deems it is time.

How has it come to this?

9

There was a star riding through clouds one night, and I said to the star, 'Consume me'

Dr Ahmed smiles, doctor-kind and knowing, straight at Connie. Holds up a syringe. 'To ease the pain,' he soothes. Someone in the audience gasps. Is that her Cliff? She does not know; still she tries to find him, cannot. He cannot have abandoned her, at this crucial moment, he cannot be leaving her here. This is terrifying, she wasn't expecting anything like it, she feels so cruelly exposed, wronged, humiliated; the spell is snapped. 'Show us all how brave you are,' the doctor whispers close, just to her, holding high the instrument for all to see. 'It's just like getting your ears pierced. Show us how much you want this.'

And at that moment Connie catches sight of Cliff, by the door the servant entered, smiling, willing her on and needing this and she succumbs once again, latches onto the surrendering, grabs at it; pushing her cunt out, out, as far as it can go, ready to receive, for him, yes, the magnificent depths of her love . . . for this has brought them both alive . . . she will be consumed by it, transformed, someone else entirely . . . for him . . . his creation, toy, fascination, his means of being flooded with life; she shuts her eyes, wills it, the slipping into something else. For after all, she is the good wife, everyone knows this.

A local anaesthetic first but still the pain is searing

as the first hole in Connie's flesh is punched through but she does not cry out, she does not, knowing Cliff doesn't want that . . . but at the second piercing, oh God – it cannot be helped: a piercing scream tears the night.

This is not an act.

Blackness . . . she slumps onto the soft mink . . . the relief of the oblivion. All soothing, velvety dark, all quiet.

10

Why are women . . . so much more interesting to men than men are to women?

He has asked her to write it down, all of it, the raw, unvarnished depths; the great and astonishing cistern of her lusts. Cliff needs to know, urgently now, and in a supreme act of love Connie has done so. She has stripped herself bare, violently, with moving vulnerability, just for him; she has unleashed her deepest, innermost thoughts. And to a man. A trusted confidant, when women rarely reveal the rawness of this vivid underbelly. To anyone. This, their secret life. Which is rarely given life.

'He is a man of decidedly singular and specific wants.'

Clifford is confined to a wheelchair. A skiing accident at Klosters, two years into their marriage. And in the gilded unliving of this feted Notting Hill couple – the ex-Goldman banker and his fragrant, former model wife – this, now, is what keeps them tremulous. Connected. There is no physical sex between them. There cannot be because of Cliff's condition. It is all, now, in the mind. It is all deeply secret display and withholding and commanding and surprise and play – and truth, audacious truth. And it is better now than it ever was, when their marriage was conventional, when Cliff was whole; it is as if a grainy black and white movie has burst into Technicolor life. Because one night – upon hearing his grief-stricken frustration as he tried stirring his deadened penis into stiffness and could not – Connie took up her husband's Mont Blanc pen and spilled, courageously, her innermost thoughts.

What she really wanted. What she did not. Because Cliff had asked. Had begged for anything that could help them both.

How to love a new husband whose very manhood has been suddenly snatched? She would not leave him although many in their honeyed west London circle expected it. She'd get a grand payout, she was still young and attractive and could move on to someone else, set herself up in a Portobello mews and open a bespoke chocolate shop – but they all underestimated the Cornwall girl. For Connie has a lapdog sense of good in her. Of decorum, of duty, of Christian respect. There was pity there too, and a desire for sudden usefulness after years of being the trophy ornament to various men, the girlfriend everyone wanted to fuck. She would not leave her crippled husband, she could not. She would become a different type of wife now, devote herself entirely to Cliff, do whatever it took to have him lead as normal a life as possible, with normal wants.

Or abnormal. As she soon found out. Because it worked. Like a match struck into darkness it sprang Clifford back into life. He became a man again, with a man's vociferous lust. And she was pleased, so pleased, at that.

11

Women have served all these centuries as looking glasses possessing the magic and delicious power of reflecting the figure of man at twice its natural size

Cliff knew little of Connie until the accident. Their sex life had been uninspired. Connie loathed kissing her husband but had never told him this. It was like he was trying to eat her lips; she hated his breath, how he ate, the clicking of his jaw as he masticated, how he brushed his teeth. He made love with an utter absence of tenderness, as if it had never been shown, taught, as if he had no idea what this was. He took a long time to come, too long, and the whole process veered, often, into tedium and hurt. Connie sometimes thought she could die in that time, as he was grinding away, unproductively, gratingly; she could not bear it, with every pore of her body she could not. She never told him this. He pawed her breasts with an absence of finesse, her nipples remained stubbornly soft. Nothing worked.

Nothing had ever, really, worked. But Clifford Carven the Third was a man set, there was no point in trying to veer him into something else. An American of supreme self-confidence and little self-doubt; a golden boy, an only child from east coast wealth who'd spent a silkily entitled lifetime getting his way and thinking little of anyone else, because he didn't have to. Handsome, in that robust, blue-blooded American way, of rude, patrician health, as if his entire upbringing consisted of daily vegetables, energy-boosting drinks and the cleansing salt from wooden-decked Cape Cod yachts. Handsome, yes, but cold with it; his face as it aged falling away into hard angles and planes, the leanness and ruthlessness of a competitive cyclist now in him. But for Connie, at the start, he was a promise of something else. For her, for her children. A higher dynamism, perhaps. They were a golden couple and they knew it.

Connie had never come with him. She never told him that. In fact, she had never had an orgasm in her life. Her husband wouldn't know because he never asked. He made love selfishly, with little thought for the recipient. Always had, because he had the air of a man who had never had a woman say what she really, actually, might want. It was too late, Connie didn't try, didn't care enough. And she knew that satisfying sex in terms of a woman was only one small aspect of the fullness of married life, and fleeting or absent for most, so she contented herself with gleaning satisfaction from the other parts. A gaggle of bankers' wives and girlfriends around her for shopping weekends to Paris, pedicures in a gossipy line at the Cowshed, movie nights at the Electric. A show house of careful beauty, the former residence of the Portuguese ambassador. A manicured garden of clenched formality. Sushi parties for the girls, book club hostings, charity lunches, church fundraisers. Glittering dinner parties for fifty, Christmas drinks, Guy Fawkes barbecues, work dos, anything and everything to mask the terrible silence of the two of them, alone, like a shroud upon them both.

And then the accident, and the marriage was shifted onto another path. Cliff's pumped charisma gone, to be replaced by something else: a simmering snippiness and cruelty brought about by a sheer sense of raging misfortune, Connie suspects; it's something that, pre-accident, never seemed to surface. Her duty: to soften all that, to set things right, however she can. She has a purpose now.

Yet, yet. There is a woman she once knew and she gazes at her occasionally as though through thick, opaque glass; can't touch her, grasp her, be her. That woman is free, fearless, blazing, bold. She is young, her younger self. The lust for losing her virginity surprises her even now, how badly she'd wanted to be rid of it. Yet ever since she has felt disconnected from the sex act, as if she was looking at it, every time, from the ceiling; observing it, wondering, flinching. *This* is what it's all about? Surely not. The horror of sex not her way – not the emboldened way it always was in her head – was the first great shock of her adult life.

The men, again and again, who seemed so indifferent to who she really was; who just didn't want to know, ask. It's me, she was raging inside, this is who I am. She grazed upon sex through boyfriend after boyfriend; never gulped it complete, never swallowed it whole. Watched, intrigued, always watched; no one could pene-trate her careful, observing, inscrutable shell. Then she married Clifford in the Seychelles in front of one hundred guests they'd flown in specially for the occasion and she stepped into, seemingly effortlessly, a world of ridiculous wealth: of subterranean screening rooms and swimming pools, of separate his and her massage rooms, summer as well as winter walk-in wardrobes, four cars (one just for the motorway alongside three vintage Porsches), of FedExed luggage, multiple help, ordering off the menu, daily blow-dries, museum-quality art. Like many rich wives, she rarely looked happy; no, that wasn't the word for it: she looked collected, smooth, in a uniformly thin, carefully blow-dried, thoroughbred kind of way.

And it was only when Connie was needed that something like love – as far as she knows what love is – uncurled. The accident tipped their sex life into something else. Because Cliff gouged out – patiently, gently, beseechingly – the very marrow of his impenetrable wife. It had become the trigger that now tipped him into someone else. To see her so wanton, transformed, bared, cracked, made him focus on another, made him forget.

Her girlfriends have no idea of any of this. A listener rather than a talker, a receptacle for everyone else's angst, Connie is extremely good at maintaining a secret life.

12

*Often on a wet day I begin counting up; what
I've read and haven't read*

'I want you to read. I want you to tell me what works.'

So. The good wife, eager to facilitate, is flushed by a new sense of purpose. Reading above and beyond her creamy bankers' wives book club with their Booker winners and Harvill challenges and occasional star guest who lives close. Reading at home, flushed, in the middle of the day, straddled firm on cool steel. A strumming hand. Drinking from an untapped well of words that tingle her up; that initiate, transform, exhilarate, unlock. It is writing that elicits a visceral response like no other words ever have; speaking directly to her in a secret language, woman to woman. To have such potency, as an artist, to elicit such a belly-churning jolt. Only connect, of course. It is said Renoir painted his pictures with his penis and Connie now seeks the words women write with their vaginas. Needs their vulnerability and their truth: as ugly and thrilling and complex and excruciating and scarred as her own. She finds it. Cliff, too. In a world she would never dare talk about with her friends, for she knows too much of it now; mustn't give herself away, mustn't break the spell of it.

And so the two of them began, alone. Tentatively. With blushing honesty. An exploratory spirit. Shared books, the enchantment of them, for it *is* an enchantment. Connie reads fast, her breath shallow, her belly dipping; breathing in deep the liberation of these new texts like a corset unloosed. The journeying progresses into the reality of words suddenly slammed down – a husband summoned, a wheelchair straddled, a Mont Blanc pen whispered into an anus that has never been penetrated; by night the Box visited and by day Coco de Mer; Brazilians are performed at home by a black man of satiny physique; there are collars and handcuffs, blindfolds and belts. The shame dies fast because the new world unlocked is so spectacularly different, trans-porting, vivifying; yet Connie had been stolidly sexually active for at least a decade before all this.

It's as if Cliff senses that this is now the one way to entrap his beautiful, slippery, inscrutable wife, to bind her tight to his new life; it's as if he isn't quite confident of anything else. And so Connie is reeled in, resisting, but caught nonetheless. Complicit at every step.

All the stops on her life at such a young age, except this, vividly this. Cliff's goal: to gouge out the – aston-ishingly different – woman underneath. *I take you to be* . . . but what he discovers over these days following the accident is that she is actually, exhilaratingly, quite someone else. And gradually, over time, dear, sweet Connie Carven of the carefully blow-dried hair and Vivier shoes – faithfully handing out her Bibles at the door of St Peter's every second Sunday of the month – has slipped beyond her calcified adult life into a glit-tery, secret new existence that steals, spectacularly, her nights. Her husband found the key, at the height of cruel misfortune; his singular triumph in a time that seemed utterly absent of it.

Connie felt *needed* with all this. Thrillingly. Gratefully.

Don't we all have a universal desire to be needed in our lives? That basic human want. Cliff had a plethora of helpers – drivers, housekeepers, cleaners, personal valets, cooks – to smooth his way in every other respect. Except this one; the one that plumed him into feeling like a man once again.

But now he wants something else. The logical next step. An overwhelming desire to share his triumph with a select few, to trumpet it. He's that secure with the velvety ropes now binding this relationship tight.

13

*Why, if one wants to compare life to anything,
one must liken it to being blown through the
Tube at fifty miles an hour – landing at the
other end without a single hairpin in one's hair!*

He puts her to bed like a child. They do not sleep together. They never sleep together. Connie is up high, in the vast attic room, her choice. Her wonder room. Full of twigs and shells and sticks and cones, fossils, bones, sketches, books. Hand-stitched quilts from Victorian Ireland, battered fishing tins of wondrously mottled green, Edwardian rods from the Cornish coast. The windows are never shut so every night Connie can drink the night, the moon, the sky; and by day the melancholy cries of gulls that speak of London's great maritime past and sing her home. The room has a lift, at Cliff's insistence, but he never lingers, for this space represents a wild side of his wife he never quite trusts. Because it can't be bought. She is a woman raw in this eyrie and he doesn't want this aspect of her anywhere else. No leakage of any of this world – raw, battered, found grubbily off the street – is allowed into the rest of the house.

The rest: a bone house, no warmth. Interior-designed within an inch of its life. Audacious chairs, thick art books (never opened), oatmeal throws and broad, boastful art. This, of course, is what's photographed.

Cliff kisses Connie on the cheek, kisses his thanks for the magnificence of the night. She turns from him, sleepily; feels the virgin weight raw between her legs.

Does not know how many hands inspected as she lay there unconscious, in that theatre; she can feel an ache, a fulsome sullying. Was Clifford watching from the wings? Who, eventually, inserted the padlock? Who snapped it shut? With what sense of ceremony? She does not know. Any of it.

But it is there now, securely locked and suddenly, in the quiet, Connie is unstoppably up on all fours, a pillow under her, grinding the fresh, cold heaviness into her. The drug of it, the drug; never mind the bleeding, the six weeks of getting used to fresh piercings, the endless twisting of the hoops, the careful tending of it. She is back. It is worth it. Further and further along the path. She will do it all, all, for moments of exquisiteness like this when her body succumbs so beautifully and magnificently and powerfully and she is in awe of it, all of it; how she becomes, so completely, someone else entirely; forgetting the pain and the terror and the discomfort in the blind, addictive want. Thinking now of a myriad of hands, and cocks and cunts; cool Nika, the coy driver; it is not connected with Clifford in any way; never is, never was. She comes swiftly and collapses on the bed.

Has never felt more primed in her life.

14

*For beyond the difficulty of communicating
oneself, there is the supreme difficulty of being
oneself*

Connie collects Tracey Emin, the brazen knot of her. Cliff lets her because she's 'kinky'.

'She's not kinky, she's honest,' is the retort.

The soft glare of the neon in startling corners of the house.

'I said Don't Practise ON ME.'

'I KNOW I KNOW I KNOW.'

'MY CUNT IS WET WITH FEAR.'

The latter in the shared bathroom off the main bedroom that Connie hasn't used since Cliff's accident.

On the stairs leading to her eyrie is the wiry delicacy of legs splayed, a plunged hand, a labia scurried. Reddened, raw. The titles: *Self Growth*, *Thinking About It*, and *Those Who Suffer Love*, a series of heels and ankles wide, as wide as they can be, in homage to Courbet's *L'Origine du Monde*.

Connie is drawn to Emin as she is drawn to Dickinson, Réage, Duras, Plath, for their vulnerability, authenticity, anarchy, courage, truth. Cliff just thinks she needs a fuck, quick smart. 'That'll fix her up.'

15

*It is in our idleness, in our dreams, that the
submerged truth sometimes makes its way to
the surface*

Connie wakes late into a hard light. Pain, down below. Itch. Practically, how can this work? What is happening to us all? she wonders. All this brazen new openness and honesty, all this craven, spectator want? Public figures, A-list celebs, young royals: they're all ending up at the Box at some point. Where does it go from here? The experimentation increasingly permeating the public sphere, the new nakedness, raw talk. The Brazilianed and Botoxed ladies of her book club have all read *Fifty Shades* and now discuss bondage and belts when once it was Proust and now this, her fresh little branding, yet it doesn't feel so odd. The voracious devouring of these illicit texts feels revolutionary in terms of women's reading; the dawn of a new age of . . . what? This new decadence, effulgence, feels like the tipping point of some sort, an inexorable slide into a waning like the Roman Empire's demise and Connie wonders what on earth could follow it. A flinch into extreme conservatism, perhaps, a vast reining back?

All she knows is that there is a body, a being, a confidence that dies as soon as light hits her high room and the real world intrudes. But those secret nights . . . oh, those nights.

16

*I thought how unpleasant it is to be locked out;
and I thought how it is worse, perhaps, to be
locked in*

Eleven a.m. Saturday. Breakfast together, the yellow and black room at the back of the house. Cliff chewing loudly as he reads the *FT*, masticating his egg and toast, slurping down his coffee in a loud gulp. Connie cannot bear the sounds, he is oblivious. No one has ever pointed them out to him, she is sure. It is one of those moments of utter stasis between them when her future life comes hurtling towards her suddenly, a wall of acquiescence, stillness, rot.

Cliff looks up as if he's only just realized she's there. Inclines his head. Engages. Reverses his wheelchair, a touch. Asks her to throw her silken kimono from Myla off one shoulder and come closer, right by him, to sit in the chair next to him, upright, one leg cocked: 'Let's see what that small fortune spent on yoga poses actually does for you, hmm?'

Connie complies, winces, it hurts.

He inspects, smiles a murmur, 'Good good,' snaps his paper for better viewing and returns to his reading. Connie relaxes her leg. 'Play.' Brusque, from behind the newsprint. 'Cherish the family crest. Show me. I want to see. Hear.'

Connie feels too stiff, raw. It hurts. She stops.

Silence. Stillness. Her cage and she has constructed it, of course. With her obedience, her compliance, her truth.

Cliff continues reading the paper, lost in his mergers. Connie now gazing out the window, thinking of Picasso, how he said that all women were goddesses or doormats and if they weren't doormats at the start of the relationship then he'd do his level best to crack them into it. Herself? She's never been any threat. It's why his tight, moneyed family likes her, she knows that. One of those sweet ones who will not rock the boat; a pleaser, primed for a rubbing out; instinctively his family of strong women recognized it despite the slight niggle of a gold-digger, she can sense it; but she's sure they're like that with anyone who comes into their fold.

'You will look after him, won't you?' enquired his mother, upfront, at the start. 'Yes,' Connie answered simply, 'yes of course,' even then. And she has ever since. No one's ever been afraid of her cowardice, her compliance; they all take her to be the good wife. Look after him, of course, but what about herself? Who'll look after her? She's a girl, she'll be fine, she can look after herself.

'Where do we go from here?' Connie suddenly asks into the morning quiet.

Cliff puts down the paper. Wheels his chair close. Props her leg back sternly, then the other one, and brushes a touch, admiring his handiwork; his wife's knuckles are white on the chair's rim. He does not know this. He tells her he has a new client. His voice, signalling the start of the process. A young South American, from Argentina; not a talker, a possibility, there's something cheeky and ready in him, her 'type'. A pause. There's a scenario . . . he'd like to try out. He toys with his new bauble buried between his wife's legs. Her eyes are closed, giving nothing away. Cliff talks on. A business meeting here, at home. Not now, but when she's healed, readied. He will ring for papers. His wife will volunteer to help, she is close, she knows where they are. She will enter his office, bundle in hand, wearing the shortest of her Chanel skirts, that red one, with the fringe, and her six-inch Louboutins. Then just as she hands them across the desk the papers will be dropped, the whole lot. She will bend, on all fours, and pick them up. Slowly. Searching. Her rump high and square to this stranger.

His test.

Which Cliff will watch.

'No knickers.' Connie nods, feeling the wave of complicity, the stirring, washing through her despite herself.

'Of course. And most importantly – my lovely, lovely new trinket.' He strokes it with his thumb.

'Arse high, skirt riding up.'

'Yes. I want to watch his face. See what happens next. Give you a room of your own, together. Watch what he does, what he attempts.' He tugs slightly on the padlock, she gasps. 'You'll have the key. You'll have had it all along. Under your tongue, yes. Pass it to him, please, lips to lips. I want to watch his astonishment. Him opening you. That moment of release. The trembling intimacy, the thrill, the freedom, all of it, I need to see it. What happens next . . . every orifice . . . you begging for it.'

Connie's suddenly shutting her legs down in one enormous 'but' and she's not even sure why, she's just stopped like a match suddenly snuffed. The moment's gone. Just like that. They were in tandem and now they are not. As simple as that.

Cliff doesn't realize. All is stillness, suddenly, in the careful, ticking room which has the tall clock of his great-grandfather who went down on the *Titanic*, a hero of the first class. Connie looks out the window to the tall trees of the communal garden moving in the breeze, their black tracery scratching at a pale, white sky as if trying to tear it aside. Everything feels so different in the wan light of eleven o'clock. Damaged. Wrong. All that's left for her now are bruised thighs and a dull ache. She feels suddenly skinned by her husband. Unshielded, cold, raw. Where does this all end up? Like sad little O – enslaved? Such a depleting journey for that poor, trammelled girl.

And yet . . . and yet . . . the deliciousness.

No.

17

You cannot find peace by avoiding life

'Am I meant to wear this all the time?'

The enchantment is gone, the spell broken. Connie wants it off.

'Of course not.' From behind the newspaper. 'The sleepers have to be in for a month, six weeks, and then you can put in whatever you want. Studs if you like, I don't know. Mmm, imagine that, Con? And the little padlock, well, that's just for playtime. For when I say. When I want.'

'Why do you want me to sleep with other men?' The question she has asked again, and again, and again.

The sigh. 'It gives me pleasure. But more importantly, gives *you* pleasure.' How dare he presume to know what I think, Connie muses. 'You need it now. I'm very aware of that.' He smiles, cold. 'I'm the good husband, no?'

Cliff's answer – whatever it is, on whatever day – is not enough, is never enough. He's not interested in so much, has no passion for anything around him except accumulating vast and competitive wealth – so why this? He devours his Porsche magazines, is just finishing modifying a super-yacht, collects vintage champagne, accrues spectacular bonuses and spends almost every penny of them but rarely thinks of anyone else. He unlives, with so much. Even the charity commitments are selected with careful PR advice. He has little idea of where the money's spent, 'Just none of those fucking animal liberationists, OK, can't abide their thick, braying stink.'

Cliff wants to participate with an observer's coolness, wants others to admire, covet. Draws power from envy and adulation; is smooth with it, silvery with his thatch of greying hair, buoyant. Has always seen his hedge fund clients as objects rather than people – fools, sops, muppets – and Connie wonders how far this extends into other areas of his life.

To her it means almost nothing except that she gives herself to him, as the good wife. It is a kind of love, what he allows her to do now; no, it *is* love, she tells herself. Generosity of spirit, finally, yes; to be fulfilled by other men. The small price to pay: that he be allowed to watch. Control, yes, always that, for he is a controlling man. Pure head, no belly, no heart. And she is his adornment, his most beautiful trinket, her pliancy and servitude his triumph.

Yet now this, the next step.

'That moment of release, the trembling intimacy' – what was it that Cliff had said? – *'the sudden freedom as you're unlocked, I want to watch it . . .'*

For Connie, a violent disconnect. Because all this should be with a husband, no one else. She stands, wraps the kimono around her, and without another word walks out.

18

*To me you're everything that exists; the reality
of everything*

Late February. The two of them in the communal garden. Out, out, into the flush of fresh air; the weather finally breaking, a wan light on their faces. Connie can never quite get over the rarefied world of the locked garden gate in these parts, those beautiful expanses of public space behind their iron railings that firmly keep out the public. It feels so ragingly undemocratic; every day she spies bewildered tourists rattling the lock, failing to understand, and then the dawning as someone slips past them with their electronic key and shuts the gate apologetically in their faces.

'This is private, you know, if I let you in you won't be able to get out.'

They, the keyholders, another species altogether. Co-owners of one of the most ravishingly beautiful private gardens in London, more exquisite than any public park, three acres shared among a select coterie of homeowners whose villas smugly necklace the expanse. Guy Fawkes effigies are dressed in discarded Burberry at the annual bonfire, there are nannies with Stella McCartney baby bags, the blazers and straw hats of some of the best pre-preps in London, the gracious elderly with easels and the rubbish bins brimming with empty Moët bottles. The French and the Italians, the Aussies and the Yanks are slowly pushing the old Brit money out. Through a rusting art nouveau gate Connie and Cliff's manicured private garden of white pebbles, box hedges and bamboo opens out to beauty, all beauty, of a fundamentally British kind. A secret land. Rolling lawns and languid willows, roses and bluebells and oaks as well as gravel walks and tennis courts, a playground and sandpit for children, an outdoor gym for adults. But alongside all this, the secret parts: the scruffy, reclusive pockets of wildness with obscure Victorian urns and rotunda follies, little moments rarely stumbled upon that are deliberately, audaciously overgrown, pure nature unleashed. A blanket of removal seems to fall over gardens like this when you enter them. A feeling of peace and space and serenity and expansiveness that no one else in this city has; a great, privileged exhalation amid the cram of life.

Cliff has been carried out to his spot under the great northern oak, Connie beside him on the bench with her Saturday *Times* and *Telegraph*, the juicy bits, and her guilty read, the *Mail*, because she must. She can sense the pent-up rain contained in the very walls of the houses and the fences, the bark of the trees, the soil. Smell the soaking, months and months of it, pluming the ground. Notting Hill, indeed the entire country, has been engorged with rain and it is as if the very earth is now spewing forth its dampness.

Connie looks up from her papers: a rogue person has got in, she doesn't know how; he is wearing a hoodie which she instinctively shrinks from and he has that unhealthy pallor so many of them have, as if they've never eaten a vegetable in their lives. He is walking around, rapt, gazing at this other world just as Connie gazed at it, incredulous, once. She draws a touch closer to Cliff. Doesn't like the rogue world intruding on her life, has grown unused to it; the world of the garden represents a vast bunkering down. Yet this is an area that was heavily targeted during the war and alongside some of the most expensive real estate in the world are council estates on old bomb sites; it all rubs up too close for Connie's liking, far too close. She can read the stares as she slides into her darkened cars . . . envy, sneer, menace, hate.

Clifford catches her gaze, winks; 'You'll be all right.' Exiles both, anonymous here, as two people neither born nor raised in London and with no family close. She is sure both couldn't do what they're now doing, in their secret life, in their own places of birth. Here they can revel in the anonymity of the exile, far, far away from the anaesthesia of the known. Here, she is someone else.

The interloper is gone. Connie rises from her bench, needs a walk. She ends up in a wild pocket, in a circle of black urns, an odd, funereal remnant from the Victorian imagination. Here the gardener has somehow managed to coax shy snowdrops to grow and she smiles at that; a touch of home. She feels far, far away from the rhythms of the earth here in London. Nothing feels natural, everything is intervention. She longs to get back to the wild land, to air laden with sea. Longs to roll herself in sand again like she used to as a child, to cleanse, to restore herself. Needs a basting in roaring sunlight.

Connie looks back at her man, his face full to the feeble sunlight heralding spring, his useless ankles vulnerably thin as they poke from his Ralph Lauren corduroy. She knows the Brits always looked at her American as someone to be laughed at and admired and feared in equal measure. His energy was the future. His grasp, boldness, affront. The way he showed off his excessive wealth, revelled in it, laughing at the Brits with their scruffy, faux modesty, their battered old cars and couches covered in dog hairs and sense of detached quiet and bewilderment (which was anything but, he saw right through it). Cliff would drop fifty thousand on alcohol at a restaurant without thinking anything of it; would fly out planeloads of partygoers to the south of France and hire an entire village for it. Connie, ever faithfully beside him, grew quickly addicted to this way of living – loved the sparkly, unthinking splash of it.

Cliff would never be one of them, all the Brits around them knew it; it was amusing and threatening at once. He never bothered to weave himself into the rhythms of their world, his allegiance had always been to his kind. Connie was so attracted to his otherness at the start, the difference of his energy, power, his booming voice and confidence; the animal dynamism so naked and thrilling and blunt.

He's someone else, now, with his dead ankles. She cannot abandon it.

19

Arrange whatever pieces come your way

Connie's father gets the train up from Cornwall, where he lives with her mother in genteel retirement in a manor house on a cliff by the sea. Over brunch in the Electric Club he strokes his youngest daughter behind the earlobe, just as he always has. She's getting thin, too thin. He's a former diplomat, a great walrus of a man of huge appetites and a roaring laugh, endlessly astounded that he sired such a graceful slip of a thing so late in life. Yet he's worried now that his princess, his Neesie, is becoming a demi-vierge, a half-virgin, and tells her so.

'Oh, Daddy!' Connie scoffs. 'I'm fine. Honestly.'

'The world is supposed to be crowded with possibilities, but they narrow down to pretty few in most people's experience. I worry for you, I really do.'

Connie looks out through the curtain of chains to scruffy Portobello Road below them, bustling with its vegetable carts and impatient cars, its idling tourists, pushchairs, bicycles. Possibilities in life? Hers. Now. None.

'My life is very full, Daddy. Cliff needs a lot of help.'

'Do you ever think about children, Neesie?'

'What do you mean?' she snaps.

'Having them. You're so young, you've got your whole life ahead of you. It's a . . .'

'What, Dad?'

'Waste. Your slick Yank has no use for you at all now, as far as I can see. He's entirely wrapped up in himself. Always has been. Now more than ever. You're wasting away, child. So pale, thin, and you were such a bonny thing once. What has he done to you?'

Connie's nostrils flare in annoyance, as they always have, since she was a child, when her father presumes too much.

'We're happy, Dad. As we are. I'm his wife and I have a job to do. A very important one. Now more than ever. Only I can help him, only me. I've become crucial to him in a way that's impossible to explain.' End of conversation.

'Oh, love,' says her father, and calls for the bill, which she snatches up, and he lets her, as they always do. They walk out arm in arm, laughing despite themselves, too fond of each other for anything else.

20

*They went in and out of each other's minds
without any effort*

'It's time, my love, to play.' The pen whispering Connie awake, signalling a falling, a submitting, a surrendering to the trance that will lead to goodness knows what.

'Yes.'

'Tomorrow?'

'Yes. Quick. Please.'

Cliff senses a new restlessness in his wife. A jittery, unvoiced agitation. It needs addressing. He has been neglectful in that department, is brought up sharp. Of course it's time. It's been too long. As for Connie, she needs to be needed again, needs purpose. Fast.

That afternoon, after the car has seen her father off to Paddington Station, she is prepared. The sleepers are gently worked through their tiny holes. The padlock is threaded through. Clicked shut by Cliff. She moans. Toys with the object's weight, its resistance. The thought of it. Closes her legs on it. Expectation blazing under skin.

'The release . . .' he murmurs, smiling secrets into her eyes. 'For me, for you, for us.'

Thrumming, all evening; exquisitely tuned.

21

*To let oneself be carried on passively is
unthinkable*

The red skirt with the fringe, the six-inch Louboutins, no knickers. All according to plan.

The stranger has arrived. The intercom rings.

Papers are needed; Connie takes the bundle in her arms. Deep breath. Rolling her muscles upon her secret. Ready. She opens the office door, softly. Cliff, expectant, sitting at his desk that was Napolean Bonaparte's once and is methodically neat. A man, his back to her, a stiff white collar of a very expensive shirt, a nape. In the past she has fallen in love with a mere nape of a neck, the bend of a wrist, the kink of a hip, it is all it has taken and she is gone. Once.

Connie walks straight up to her husband's desk, leans over – and hands the papers across.

Cliff's astonished face.

'Can't,' she mouths, wincing, retreating.

The nape is wrong, the moment, the intimacy that should be a husband's and no one else's, the whole confused lot of it. The spell of enchantment is snapped.

Connie leaves without looking at the stranger's face. Churning. Cliff cannot control such a privacy, he can't choose it, can't. Her mind has taken over, it has triumphed; her body is in retreat. In fraught air she backs back. Lost.

Cliff too, bewildered, but in a meeting stuck. 'I – where was I?' He smiles benignly to his guest.

22

When people are happy they have a reserve upon
which to draw, whereas she was like a wheel
without a tyre

Connie walks up the grand staircase, slowly, carefully. She feels like a pane of glass with a thousand hairline cracks: one push will shatter her. She will not be broken, she will not. Her tread is so careful, contained, her back stiff. Onward she walks, onward.

To her room, its windows slammed shut by cleaners barked at by Cliff to keep in the house's heat. Connie flings the panes wide and the cold rushes in and she collapses, belly down, on her bed. She remains there for the rest of the day and deep into the night. Her vocation of serving – submission – is not enough. No. Is meant to be enough. That is her role, as wife.

Everyone has a universal desire to be needed. How does Cliff need her? As his perversion, plaything, pet. That's it. How much pleasure will she give the others of his choosing? How far will she go? For in the upended way of their world that is the proof of her love for him now: how voluminously she will submit. How removed she is from that girl he first knew. The easy blusher, in the Peter Pan collars and knee-length skirts. She stares at her Louboutins kicked off by her bed, their ridiculously high heels that bind her to her servitude. What woman would ever design a constraint, a buckling, an absurdity, as cruel as those?

And how often has she readily stepped into them.

A visible symbol of her servitude, compliance, decadence. The girl from Cornwall with the beautiful face, bound by all this. Her walk-in wardrobes, summer and winter, her jewellery boxes, her private safe. How she has always loved her shoes and her clothes; the quickening at a singular vintage dress that fits, the Edwardian necklace, the deco cuff, the Stephen Jones hat – grabbed! – and so often now. The thrill of which has never passed. Complicit, in all of it.

Rain comes. The windows stay wide. Usually Connie feels cocooned within that sound but tonight she feels pummelled by it. The wind is high, haranguing her as if pushing her away, far away, to somewhere else. Gradually it all clears, the sky is orange as it always is, the light pollution scattering a proper, rich, weighty dark; the dark of the land, the untrammelled earth. Water drips from the eaves, endlessly drips, deep into the early hours; it feels like her life leaking away, in wakefulness and worry. The whole house of cards has come tumbling down, just like that; she has lost the sexual urge, just like that, with Cliff, with any man.

He does not come, of course, he would not. She has humiliated him, stepped out of order, done what he did not want. And meanwhile she has surfaced into something else.

A new land, a strange new life, not sure what. No ballast to it, that's all she knows.

23

He thought her beautiful, believed her impeccably wise; dreamed of her, wrote poems to her, which, ignoring the subject, she corrected in red ink . . .

'Would it perhaps be a good thing if you had a child by another man? Con? What do you think?'

Dinner, the next night. Cliff thinking aloud through thick silence, trying to ensnare his wife with talk, to work out this new person; and there is Connie, all changed, flinched, hearing him as if from afar, as though through an old diving helmet, a weight stifling, airless, wrong.

'You'd think we'd be able to arrange this sex thing as we arrange going to the hairdresser, wouldn't you? In this day and age . . .' Cliff is now snapping out his thoughts. 'Since some fucking trees on a ski slope – that shouldn't have been there in the first place – have given us a checkmate, physically, in that department.'

He is talking at Connie, not with her, as he does, he always does. 'I don't know,' she is saying, 'I don't know,' unable to articulate anything of her new, strange roar to him, her silent roar. A weary yearning, a dissatisfaction has started in her but he cannot see it and she does not expect him to. It's all talk, all nothing, a wonderful display of nothingness, Connie thinks as she looks around her at all their careful objects that were procured by the interior designer, so tastefully placed, so exquisitely photographed, so sucked of life. There is no love behind any of it, no passion, no shared stories, no mess or mistakes, not even the shard of a fight. *Because they don't care enough*, she thinks. Neither of them. Not a single thing here has been picked out by either of them, not even the family portraits in silver frames crowding a sideboard from Churchill's family home. A child? Into this?

Cliff does not want one, never has, a new creature who would interfere so meddlingly with everything he's got. He would lose control, what he fears more than anything; he's always conveyed that; it's too seismic a shift, too slippery and uncontainable for such an ordered life. Or perhaps he has a child somewhere else, has always had one. He works long hours, is a fair bit older, could cram a lot into all his time spent apart from her.

Connie doesn't care enough.

She does not respect this world. He has no idea of this. She would not want her own child to follow in Cliff's footsteps. A banker? Whose sole purpose is to be fêted in *Forbes*, to work his way up the rich list? Please. It's all about vanquishing everyone else; if colleague X acquires 200 acres in Oxfordshire, they must have 300. If colleague Y has four cars they must have five and a multi-car, underground basement garage to house them. It is all display, ridiculous plumage. The most robust bonus, the most exquisite house, the cinema room and the servants' quarters, the predictably lavish milestone birthdays in exotic places, the paintings, the cutlery, the crockery, glassware, wife. It is all so predictable, and utterly of a type; like homosexual men they must follow each other meticulously in the way they dress, what they acquire, how they display their wealth, act. And Connie is chafing, chafing at the bit.

All around her are bankers' wives having a fourth child, for even that is competitive, the bigger family for the artfully smug Christmas card photo, the new mode of accessorizing; four because they have the funds and the help and the ease to do it, four because look at us, we fuck a lot. Clifford wants other men to envy him, as simple as that; but not in terms of the child-gaggle, he's often conveyed that. He doesn't like anyone's child – despite having four godchildren – they're all too rude, loud, obnoxious, spoilt. It's all a great and ugly noth-ingness and for Connie, in this moment, to accept the great nothingness of life seems to be the end of living.

'Con, Con, what is it you want? Speak to me.'

But she can't. Because she does not know herself. Uncertainty, doubt, something like hate has cut through her world like a shark; scattering the enchantment of the secret nights.

24

I am rooted, but I flow

Mid March. Connie on the garden bench next to Cliff. Their faces full to the first proper sun of the season, pinnacles of light pricking them into a waking. It is like being soothed inside a rarefied enclosure here, behind its tall black bars, removed from the mess and the muck of the world. Cliff especially loves it, away from dispiriting Notting Hill Gate with its steely pollution you can taste in your mouth, its riff-raff of people, churning crowds, grimly unbeautiful buildings. All grey! Grey! Tired! Washed out! And the little people, the great seething mass of them, can't even discern it. Then this, so magically, secretly close. Nothing lets in the world here and he is extremely grateful for it.

A man walks past on the gravel, pushing a wheelbarrow. He doffs his flat cap at Cliff in a quick, deferential nod, flicks eyes at Connie, nothing more. Cliff barely notices.

'Who is that?' she asks, watching as the new man rakes a damp slush of leaves; his hands curiously elegant as they grasp the rake.

Cliff shrugs. 'The new gardener? He was here before, apparently, for years, then had a bit of trouble with some shrew of a wife. Moved away. Is now back. Johnnie told me. He's good, apparently. Mel or something. God knows.' Johnnie being a neighbour a few doors down, a fellow banker, a rare Brit in these parts.

Connie gazes after this new man, suddenly alert. He's in a T-shirt, unusual for this time of year, winter's chill not yet past. He's in a T-shirt as if he doesn't care for the cold, doesn't feel it, or wants the brace of it shivering him up. An animal energy, a difference. A shock of black hair. Pale skin. A face that would shadow by early evening and she's always loved the virility of that. A body gracefully lean, taut; not from the gym but from constant hard work. Grubby hands from whatever he's been doing with the earth. Dirt under the nails. A swipe of mud across his face. From the land, with the land, quick and at ease with it, in the way no one else around here is. So alone, but so sure of himself, apart; contained, uninterested in them, in any of the odd creatures who inhabit this place. Connie has a calibrated awareness, behind her *Times*, for he is like a sudden rush of a threat out of nowhere.

And he does not notice her one bit.

But there is a shine in him. It is called self-sufficiency. A pure lack of need. Of envy. Of this strange, jittery, out-of-kilter world around him, these people, their money, their ways, any of it. Connie stares after him.

Cliff does not notice.

25

What is the meaning of life? That was all – a simple question; one that tended to close in on one with years, the great revelation had never come. The great revelation perhaps never did come. Instead, there were little daily miracles, illuminations, matches struck unexpectedly in the dark; here was one

Later. A strange growly mongrel of a day, short flurries of snow then pregnant grey then brief rain then snow once again. Now it is clearing and Connie is out, again, in the deserted wild place, the garden's most secluded part. Walking stills her, brings her down into quiet; it has always been like this. Here, where nature has stolen back and the obedience of the show garden is utterly wiped, here, where all is immoral, rampant, untamed. She's not sure why, she's just needing to be alone and is holding her palm flat to the looming trunks, here, and here, breathing deep their stillness and wisdom and stoicism and quiet, the great moving strength of them.

A sound, below her, one small chirp. A tiny bird, at her feet, quite crushed. Grasping onto life. Dropped from up high, or attacked perhaps. Connie lifts the small beating heart of it in her palm, blood from the beak and down a wing. She doesn't know what to do. It's getting dark. Cliff will hate it at home. Blood, noise, mess, imminent death. Everything he can't stand. Barely knowing what she is doing, she makes her way to the gardener's grace-and-favour cottage, a sturdy work pony of a dwelling, in the north-east corner of the garden, cradling the fading life.

It's a tiny scrap of a place, meanly proportioned, ripe for damp. In fact she can smell the walls holding in the rain, can smell it clamouring to get out. Ivy snuffs the light from most windows; he would have to stoop to get inside. It always strikes her that Victorian dwellings like this were constructed coldly and deliberately to keep the inhabitants in their narrow places, to stop them from aspiring in any way to the heights. Nothing is small-scaled in her life, nothing; it is all high ceilings and vast ball-rooms and pendulous lights, excessive cinema rooms, bold diamonds, towering heels, wide cars.

She knocks. No answer. The door is slightly ajar. She swings it wide and calls out. 'Hello?' Steps inside. Indifferent furniture. Cobbled together from unloved places, no cherishing in any of it. Faded floral print on the walls, smoke-licked. Nowhere the sprightliness of a woman's touch. Then she sees him, through the kitchen, bent over the old stone tub of a sink. Shirt gone, splashing water over his chest, face; freshening up.

He turns. With a calm, searching gaze he turns. Stands there, waiting. He makes her feel shy. She blushes, sweat scuttling across her skin like too much chocolate too quickly gulped. Gazing at him – his nakedness – has hit her in the middle of the body.

But she cannot show any of it of course.

'I . . .' She holds out the bird, at a loss. In the bowl of her hands, a mess of blood and feathers and a racing heart.

'What have you got there then?' his accent, the strange sing of it. The practised boom to cut across the weather, speaking of another place, world, ancestry, life.

'I found this . . . by the trees.'

'And what am I meant to do with it?' His tone detached, cool, as he towels himself dry.

'I don't know.'

He comes close, inspects. 'The sky's all over the place, it's throwing a party at the moment. Your little friend won't last the night outside.'

He's laughing at her. Is he laughing at her? Connie will not be deflected. 'Could you keep it, maybe, perhaps?'

'It won't last much longer inside. But if I must . . .' And in one swift, gentle movement he extracts the dying bird from the cup of her hands and Connie knows in that brush of a touch that there is tenderness in him, and the sky, and the earth, he is touched by it all still; he would move like an animal in her, she just knows, it would be peaceful and different and repairing and right. It strikes her in that moment, like the flare of a match, that here is a soul strong with a simpler, grounded, utterly removed way of life to all this, around them both; it is strong in him, a mode of survival, a necessary distancing. It is utterly compelling.

And he does not notice her. She is one of a type.

But, but. Delight licks Connie behind the ear. A shiver of a touch. Her insides pull, contract. Still he discerns nothing of her churn; he turns, with the bird, and she knows it is her cue, she is dismissed. 'I'll see what I can do, ma'am.' She is done, it is time to go.

'Thank you. Mel?'

'Yes, Mel.' Not looking up.

Connie stares back at him; for a moment, she lingers and he doesn't even realize, so busy is he placing the bird in a cereal bowl with a scrap of tissue around it. A man so content, self-sufficient, alone. Not playing the game, any game. But they all play the game. All want the money, the connection, the acknowledgement. Except him. Her husband wouldn't see him, note him, in any way; Mel is part of the great seething mass of people who are there for his benefit and utterly unnoticed. He has no curiosity and Connie always thought that people without that are like houses without books – unsettling. To have bound her life to a man so narrow! So oblivious of the wonders of life! Cliff would be the type who would tear the wings off a fly, and she feels instinctively that Mel would not, it is as simple as that. It's odd how you can sense these things from a first conversation, the knowing as sharp as a flick knife. Yet she married him. So desperate for the settling, the security, so afraid. Of what?

Connie takes her leave, her heart singing from a strange haunting, brightness bleeding from a swiftly shutting sky as she brusques her way home.

Home. Such a generous word for such a shell of a place.

26

The older one grows, the more one likes indecency

Cliff could never choose this moment, never dare to presume. No man ever could. The mysterious alchemy of attraction, that moment of combustion when all else is forgotten, rubbed out. The animal desire to fuck one person, just one, with driven intent; and utterly, completely, with every bone in your body, not another. The men over the years never got that. Thought they could bend her, change her, break her down, but it is there from the first moment or it is not. Just as they never got that Connie wanted absolutely no talk over the lovemaking, ever; for she needed to imprint her particular narrative upon the process, be alone with her own, quite separate scenario in her head.

That, of course, was one thing that Cliff did come to understand – that he had become a facilitator, nothing else. In their grand and complicit experiment.

But now this.

27

*The world wavered and quivered and threatened
to burst into flames*

The moon is the colour of old bone that night as Connie stands bold, bared, in front of her full-length mirror. The Anglepoise lamp is glaring fully at her nakedness. She looks at herself, in coldness, in dismay. How odd the human body is in hard light. Frail, ugly, vulnerable, breakable, freckled and crumpled and dimpled; pulsingly primed for its biological purpose, as if it exists for that and that alone and she shivers at the thought.

She cups falling breasts. Something is slackening yet she is still young. It is the thinness, she is too thin, wilfully; the beautiful bounce and ripeness of her youth has fallen away. Now, skin and bone. Not sexy, no, absolutely not. Primed by Pilates and yoga in the edgy part of W10, which she cycles to almost daily on her black Cambridge bicycle with its wicker basket. The diligence has sculpted that sinewy, well-bred look that clothes compliment so well.

Connie thinks of all the wasted beauty of a mere ten years ago, when she had no idea of it. No idea that she was perfect, glowing, bounteous then, for all she saw endlessly, despairingly, were dimpled thighs and a pot of a belly, breasts too big and spots and endlessly obsessed over the lot of it. Tweaked, burst, dyed, shaved, starved and plucked, relentlessly trying for something better, something else. She always dreamed of an A-cup, for her little Jane Birkin Ts, the boyish, insouciant line of it. Instead, she is full-breasted with wide, wing-like, child-bearing hips she is constantly trying to flatten down. Make disappear. Never understanding why men would go for all that when women like her wanted something else entirely; constantly fighting cruel nature to attain it.

'So long as you can forget your body, Connie, you're happy,' laughed Lara once, catching her checking her reflection in the car window, and sucking in her belly, before she entered the house. But Connie can't, not yet, she's imprisoned by it. She eats little and her chest is becoming scrawny, the bones showing too much, her cheeks hollow. The wrinkles will come faster this stringent way, she knows; sees it on friends slightly older and just as scrawny and then the Botox begins, of course, that uniform, terrified face. Blaring the hatred of self.

Lara abandoned her body years ago, at forty, 'when I stopped trying to change who I was and just settled back and floated in my life. I've never looked back. Had the best sex I'd ever had, all fat and veiny and wrinkled, with a good old laugh along with it. We'd never been more adventurous, and free – because we were relaxed, we couldn't care less, and I'd found my voice.' Then the change again, within the textured journey of a woman's sexuality, the waxing and the waning throughout life. Her third marriage entirely celibate, except for the first night. 'I was glad in the end to be rid of it. I've been so productive, and content, ever since.'

Connie slips on an old nightdress from a Friday rummage in Portobello, the cream linen stiff and enveloping. She always feels safer in it, cocooned for sleep, like a child in a boarding school. She's deeply tired but knows the haranguing will come, as it always comes; the shardy wakefulness of 4 a.m. She feels now that she's in a perpetual holding pattern, wondering when and where to land or how to soar, take flight, and can't. Anything but this. Cliff, of course, is not to blame, it's just the way he is and he will never change, has never changed his entire life. She sees the little boy in him, still, too much, demanding his own way, experimenting with his flies, endlessly bending things to his will, endlessly triumphing. '*You will look after him, won't you?*' 'But what about me?' she had wanted to scream to his mother but never did, never will, endlessly the good wife.

A sense of injustice has slid into Connie, like an invisible splinter under a fingernail. It's an addling tinderbox of unfairness and duty and compassion and disquiet and it must be seen to or it will eat away at her until she implodes. She cannot see the end of it.

28

Every face, every shop, bedroom window,
public-house, and dark square is a picture
feverishly turned – in search of what?

Connie's father rings often, and her frail mother and her bossy sister, all telling her in their different way to get out, get some fresh air, fatten up; to come and see them in Cornwall, get away for a while, fill up her lungs, let the wind whip all the cobwebs out. Her old childhood room is waiting, always waiting, untouched, the high corner room facing water on two sides and no one's been in it since. Sea-licked. It was like living within the curve of a shell, for there was the constant swish of water below her, the faint hollow moan of it. Connie shuts her eyes on the endless battery of admonishment, harangued by a girl striding the great stumpy toes of high cliffs and blinking tears in the wind's snap, by her footfall sponging on a different soil and always close, the sea, the sea, the beautiful, restless width of it. She can't go back now – she dare not, for fear it will turn into a catastrophic escape – and her father knows this. He pleads for her to put on her coat and just get out of her house, at least, see the daffs in that garden square, for God's sake. 'Plant some yourself if you have to, get your hands mucky, Neesie, do something with your life.'

Connie hangs up the phone.

But they're right. A rare shaft of light beams through the window, calling her out and she must, must, for it feels like the damp and the cold have curled up permanently in her bones, nestled in their very marrow, cultivating airlessness, quietness, mould. She knows it will all be too brief, this symphony of the coming spring; one cluster of flowers bursting forth then another, and another, and she knows exactly where to find them.

She rushes out.

29

Let us not take it for granted that life exists
more fully in what is commonly thought big
than in what is commonly thought small

The wind today is roguish, playful, flurrying Connie into a smile, whooshing up her legs in a merry hello and whipping up her skirt. It's the first time in so long she's been out without a coat; the sun spines her up. The earth is opening out, she can feel it, smell its release; opening wide to the sky, to life. As always she gravitates to the wild places, the formal parts of the garden too predictable, neat, as they obediently wait for their adornment of colour.

A knocking sound.

He is there, in the thick of it, of course. Deeper Connie walks into it, deeper, until she comes across a small shack, one she knew was here, of course, but has barely registered in the past; a place for storing lawnmowers, axes, wheelbarrows, rakes.

He is chopping wood, getting rid of several large, fallen branches. Startled to see her, as if no one ever intrudes upon this, his secret place. Not happy. Wanting his solitude, the sweetness of it; needing the place where the world cannot find him and instinctively she knows this is it, she has stumbled upon it.

The churn in her belly, at the sight of him, Connie cannot help it. She sits on a rough bench by the shack, in a pool of replenishing light, watches, catches her breath. She will not be gone just yet; she wants to ask about the bird, wants to ask about so much. Mel keeps on chopping, anger tingeing it. At the intrusion, the discovery, the watching. Abruptly stops. Looks down at her, stares at her, into her. Axe loose in his hand.

'The bir—' she goes to ask but, 'You're cold,' he says over the top of it.

'Am I?' She nervously laughs.

'Your hands.'

Oh. She looks down. Orange and purple, the deep mottling on her skin, she hadn't noticed, he had. 'You need to get warm.' Something so sure, calm, authoritative; not a question but a statement and instantly acted upon. Mel disappears into the shed and emerges with a hessian sack. Rough, a bit grubby, sprouting its fibres.

The challenge.

Which she can accept, or not. Connie's cheeks patched with sudden heat. 'Thank you,' she smiles, and places the sack over her lap.

Then in that roguish whip of a day she leans back, and watches. Just that. She will not be going anywhere for some time, in the vast peace of this space, she will not give him any talk because he does not want it, his whole body is telling her that. He is so self-sufficient, comfortable, at ease with all this. Dirt on his hands, under his nails, across his cheek where he's wiped his sweat. She wants to lick it off. Smell him, snuffle into his secret furrows; it would be a healthy smell, there, under his arms, she just knows it. A working, moving, dynamic scent, close to the sky, the earth. Unlike Cliff, who likes to be shaved, clipped and trimmed, at all times, perpetually neat, devoid of smell, devoid of anything close to the animal in life. Unlike Cliff, who when walking used to appear somewhat ungainly, with his great height, this man has a natural grace. Seems almost too fine for this work. There's a beauty to him. It's held back, contained. Quiet, listening, watching, observing; not eager for the world and its traps.

Mel looks at the banker's wife watching, waiting, so open, sitting there, it is all on her face. A quizzical smile, a little flick in his loins. Dreads another woman, any one of them, with their wily, depleting, emotional ways, oh no, not now, no more messy entanglements. He needs to heal, in this garden, in this secret place. He feels that if he cannot be alone with his flintiness now, right now, in this new job, he will die; he must be left in peace. By everyone, by the world, by life. This position was meant to do it. It pays nothing but it's the peace he wants.

The sky is softening into a rare spill of gold. Connie needs to be going. She does not. She is now sitting on the bench with one leg up, crossed upon the other, like a child. The ease of it. His body is taking over; inwardly, silently, he groans. He has not been in the company of a woman for four long years, has not so much as touched one and here he is now, is in this woman's employ, technically; he knows what she wants though she will not declare it, cannot, every pore of her is singing it, he can almost smell her, it.

'It's so restful here' – she leans back – 'I'd love to come whenever I want.'

'Yes.'

Angry with her. This is his space yet as an owner she has more right to it.

'Is this private, this bit?'

'No, but I'm here a lot. Working. It would be hard to find your peace and quiet.'

She sees then how angry he is with her, how contemptuous; of her sitting here, watching, of her finding his secret place, his ring-fenced, precious inner life. A jagged silence. He does not want her, does not want a bar of her. The crippled banker's wife in her inappropriate Charlotte Olympia shoes and her Gucci shirt, one button too many undone and she only just notices it; her hand trembles over it, in embarrassment; yes, she has made a spectacle of herself.

Abruptly Connie stands. A tight smile holding the slide of her face, the fury, the hurt. She censors it with a crisp 'Goodbye'. Departs.

30

*It is a thousand pities never to say what
one feels*

Connie does not actively hate Cliff. It's just that for a long time, regrettably, there has been a physical aversion. This has never changed and never will. An aversion towards his prissy cleanliness, his obsessive shaving of not just his chin but his chest and genitals; his fear of anything too close to the earth. He has always had a physical dislike of anything too messy and mucky, long before the accident. For Connie, her antipathy towards all this was masked at the start by the sheer bullish power of Cliff, the thrill of heads turned at the collective energy of them both, the buzz in their wake. The catapulting into such a heady new life! The best booth at Locanda Locatelli, Nobu takeaway, private jets, the smorgasbord of Bond Street and champagne weekends at Claridge's; of never again having the fret of an overdrawn credit card, a straining overdraft, a crammed, stuffy Tube in her life. The exhilarating relief of all that. Oh yes, she could be bought.

She was. Deliriously. And then it was too late.

There is an extraordinary dependence now. Relentlessly. Not just sexually but with work dinners, cocktail parties, charity auctions, with constant demands to be by his side in his public life. As if Connie's youth, her vitality, her health and subservience make Cliff whole, cementing the pretence that all is normal, proceeding as planned, quiet. A life becalmed, that's how he wants it, has always wanted it. He said to her once, early on, that if one must have a relationship it should be conducted in a shade of the coolest, palest cream and no, she'd admonished, raising her bellini high, not on your life, it should be a vivid, roaring blood red! 'That settles it then, we're hopelessly unsuited,' and they'd both laughed.

The dependence has bled into all corners of Connie's life. She can't even fill a car with petrol any more, has forgotten how; hasn't stacked a dishwasher for years, paid a bill, applied her own nail polish. The colour of her life now? A brittle white.

As her husband's strange ballast. He lets her shave him or sponge him as if he were a child. Connie asked at the start of their tremulous new life, he acquiesced. It has become a habit between them. He likes her to do it naked, straddling him, his hands at her hips, in wonder, as if he can't quite believe he still has this.

She doesn't want to. She cannot stop. She must. She can't. The good wife.

31

Well, we must wait for the future to show

Early April and Connie is back, drawn inexorably back; daily the green expanse saturates her gaze from her high window, daily it calls her out. The sky hangs, its colour a battleship's waiting grey. The world is poised as if holding its breath. A storm's coming, there's electricity in the air, she can taste the thundery day sparking her alive and the rain comes suddenly, needle sharp. Connie, in the thick of it, needs to find shelter, won't make it out, runs to the wooden rotunda – too cold, exposed – dashes to the shed, hurrying along narrow paths bowered over by the garden's press. Sits on a dusty chair just inside the door and watches the world being drenched around her.

Mel comes into view, she laughs, despite herself. 'I got soaked!' she girlishly exclaims, then shuts down. At his expression. Of course, she shouldn't be in this place. 'There was nowhere else,' she adds, wiping her face.

'No matter.'

He stands beside her chair, in the doorway, in silence, watching the wet, drenched himself. She rises beside him.

'I've been to ask you . . . wondering . . . what happened to my bird?'

'Dead within the hour.'

Connie gasps.

'It put up a mighty struggle, trying to flap its way out of its mess. I held it. It was all I could do.'

'Oh.'

A tear is slipping down her face, she can't stop it, can't speak; just feels brimmed, with so much. Mel glances at her, notes. There's something so mute and hopeful and good in her, despite everything; she's better than she realizes, nicer, more than she knows. There's something spiritual, wild, of the earth to her, despite all the polish. He leans across without thinking and wipes the tear from her cheek. She smiles, lips rolled in, laughs at her silliness, 'Just a bird!' in wonder and ridiculousness. Amid the thumping rain, the canopy of slick green, his hand lingers a touch. A trickle of a caress. Blind, instinctive, whisper-soft. It drops to the dip in her neck. Lingers at the vulnerability; the soft, wild beat of it.

'You should come into the hut.' His voice neutral.

'Yes,' Connie murmurs, as if in a trance, 'yes.' There are hessian sacks, ready, waiting. On the floor. Has he laid them, for this, for what? No, surely not. There's a fluttery newness in her, a tug, a wet. Her belly, her very depths feel liquid, ready for anything or nothing, she knows now what. Connie's hand slips into her pocket; quietly, secretly, she brushes her mouth, slips something under her tongue.

'Lie here,' he says and with a quaint obedience she does. Absolutely straight, on her back, arms crossed demurely upon her chest as if she has never before done this, as if she doesn't know what to expect. Waiting, breathing snagged. He lies the supine length of her, nudging close, she can feel his strong, slow, unhurried weight, he is up on one hip and caressing her inner thighs, with such infinite tenderness, and cherishing; closer, he nudges, closer, swirls, opening her gently, so gently out, closer and closer to her core and she lies back and closes her eyes and cries out softly, just that. With gratitude, with relief. A tear slips down her temple.

'What's wrong?' he asks, concerned.

'Nothing.' She shakes her head, murmurs, 'Go on, please, don't stop.'

Reverently Mel lifts up Connie's dress, reverently he brushes her navel with a kiss. Draws down her panties, and stops, gasps. With shock, with pity, sorrow – at what he sees before him; at this poor, caged creature who's fluttered into his life – and Connie reaches up and draws him strong into a wallop of a kiss and as she does so she passes something metallic and hard from her tongue into his mouth, the tears streaming down her cheeks.

Mel stops in surprise, draws back. Retrieves a small key. Stares at it in bewilderment.

'Help me,' Connie whispers. 'I want to be alive again. Please, get rid of this padlock, get rid of all of it.'

And so he does. First the lock, then the two tiny sleepers, with sure steady hands and an infinite gentleness, the gentleness of hands used to unhooking animals from a trap. All the while shaking his head in wonder and horror that the world has come to this.

Connie is finally unlocked. She pushes herself wide, wider with release. The moment Mel enters her body is a moment of pure peace. With a sudden thrusting back he withdraws and comes quick; seed is spilled upon her stomach with a quiet, guttural groan and then a stillness plumes through him, through them both, like sleep.

They lie there listening to the rain, its slowing, the soft drip, drip, of its aftermath. They lie there with the smell of saturated, sated earth, utterly quiet with no talk. His wet, sticky body touching hers, completely unknown, and right. It is like an abandonment for them both. Of everything else in their lives, here, in this secret place.

'I thought I'd done with it for now,' Mel laughs ruefully, as if he can scarcely believe it.

'What?'

'Fucking. Women. Life.'

'Life,' Connie says wondrously, soft. 'Life,' she repeats.

His smile, arrowed into her, his smile at all of it.

32

One must love everything

Striding home across a darkened park, the gravel path an entrail of paleness to her married existence but no fear now, no dread, a tall walk. Like she's just had exhilarating sex, the power of it inhabiting her whole body. Alive again, alive, and supremely flushed with it. Life, Connie smiles, *life*, each has brought the other back into it. Mel's touch and his smell are threaded into her fingers and giggly, tremulous, she holds them to her nose, her mouth, and breathes deep.

All smiles, filled up like a glass. Feeling unshadowed at last.

And so it begins.

33

*She had known happiness, exquisite happiness,
intense happiness, and it silvered the rough
waves a little more brightly, as daylight faded, and
the blue went out of the sea and it rolled in waves
of pure lemon which curved and swelled and
broke upon the beach and the ecstasy burst in
her eyes and waves of pure delight raced over
the floor of her mind and she felt, 'It is enough!
It is enough!'*

Through April, through May, Connie's days are newly oiled, she is sprung into wakefulness. Mel's smile is rangy in her, loosening her gut. But she must wait, all the time wait, for the day's softening, for the residents to depart the park, for Cliff to be late home from work.

He's entertaining a client tonight, it'll be a lap dancing club of course, he revels in it, none of them knows how much, all that look but no touch. So, today, a possibility! An afternoon of sprightly sun, warm and replenishing, uncurling the world from its long winter sleep as if it is life itself.

Swiftly Connie looks around and enters her bower of wild branches overhanging a fragment of path, almost swallowing it complete; swiftly she is enveloped by a distant wind roar and birds somewhere close and the scurries of low animals; swiftly she flits by the peak of an old greenhouse, askew, its beautifully carved wooden apex straining from nature's clutching like a man reaching from quicksand or an earthquake-sunk church. Every gardener has left it untouched, Mel has told her, it's like a secret code between us, not to disturb it, to let the earth take over and every one of us has respected that. Cliff wouldn't, Connie had remarked in reply, if he knew he'd have it cleared, bulldozed without a thought, he's so disconnected from nature, from the earth. Can't bear it.

*　　*　　*

Flitting to the clearing, to the shed. He is there. Waiting. She pauses, cusped. A slow smile. Skittery breath.

'No one would ever catch us, would they?'

'No one ever bothers with these parts. Except wild women far too greedy for their own good,' he chuckles, gathering her up, her want. 'But no, you can relax. You just have to be careful.'

'We both do, mate.' She waggles a finger at him.

Mel giggles her to a tree, giggles her to the ground. 'Not here,' Connie laughs him away. 'Yes,' he says urgently, 'oh, yes.' His hands. A knowing, practised gentleness. As he unpeels her clothes, lifts her whole and slips off her panties, unhooks her bra at the front and exposes her breasts, softly trickles his fingers across them as if he can't quite believe it, any of it, and she surrenders to the ritual baring in silence, the lovely ritual, with all the familiar tugging and the wet. Then his hands scoop up rich, moist dirt and he rubs it over her, laughing and stroking it vast across her belly, down her arms, along her cheeks and her cunt, blooding her, cleansing her, wiping her clear of her sullied other life and then he buries his head in the very depths of her and breathes deep, deep, as if he needs her returned to this sky, this earth. Trembling, he positions himself over her. Smiles deep into her, drops; nudges, expectantly, trembles her wider and wider as she clutches him tight and as he comes, and comes, a vast peace blooms through them both. All is quiet, in the softening hour of the fading day, all still, all spent.

But no. Not yet. Who knows when next. So now Connie's hands, fresh, fevering him. Floating her lips over his body, gathering him in the wet cave of her mouth. Nudging her tongue into his ear, finding the pale clearing behind his ears, breathing a moth of a kiss, can't get enough. His smell, his breathing, the heavy heat of him her blanket, his arm flung, the pale vulnerability of his inside skin, the curve of his upper arm as bare and beautiful as a Sahara dune, the marbling of blue, the river-map of veins traced by a fingertip. The brazen roar of his sex, the thickly shouting hair of it. It's been so long since she's seen that, too used to all the shaving and clipping, all the careful, astringent, sexless men of this new world.

Mel fingers her punched holes, wondrously. So strange, cruel, barbaric. Those smooth, snaky creatures, those masters of the universe controlling the world's fate, crowing their prowess and winning, always winning and always slipping back into their ways despite the chidings, the rebukes, awarding themselves ridiculous bonuses and never pulling themselves up – yet how selfish and singular and pathetic, how oddly, vulnerably, human they all are.

'Never do this again, will you?' Mel whispers, cupping Connie protectively, can't bear the sight of it. 'You're like a halfling,' he murmurs in wonder. 'Half in this world, half in the shadows. I need to get you fully out, my wild, broken thing. Get you fixed. Promise me this will never happen again.'

'God, no.' Connie pushes his hand away, shamed, shamed at all of it, her entire, calcified, beholden adult life. 'Where's the padlock?'

'In some corner of the shed. It hasn't been touched since it was flung away.'

'I need it.'

Without a word Mel finds it, retrieves it. Connie turns it in her fingers. 'This must have cost a fortune,' she whispers, then flings it away, as far as she can, in a ritual of release to be claimed by the undergrowth and lost for ever like that steeple of the greenhouse; a relic from another age, another life. Laughter bubbles up: 'Gone, gone, all of it!' She languishes her arms behind her head, the joy geyser-high. The padlock will never be found, she will never have to set eyes on it again, she is freed.

Now they are back, curled under that tree, their bodies a jigsaw fit. A sanctity of silence, a sealing kiss. Connie is tired, swiftly, so very tired. A great calm washes through her as the day softens into dark on what feels like a momentous occasion; a shifting into something else entirely; her first utterly unfettered, utterly trusting night with a man who is on her side, at last. She nestles down into Mel and his arm wings her sudden sleeping, she is cradled in it.

34

Never are voices so beautiful as on a winter's evening, when dusk almost hides the body, and they seem to issue from nothingness with a note of intimacy seldom heard by day

Mel has gone to his cottage, Connie has followed, carefully, in her own time, in the thick dark of no one about.

'I've run you a bath,' he says, quiet, as she enters, lighting a candle in a tin holder.

'Where is it?'

'Above you.'

Connie pokes her head up a dangerously narrow wind of wooden stairs. A tiny first floor, eave-tucked. Delicious. Perfect. She climbs to it. The wooden floor creaks and bows like a saddle beneath her weight and she symphonies the wide boards with her feet and claps her hands, giggling in pure delight.

'They're old coffin lids. Surplus from Kensal Rise, I guess. Held in place by thatcher's ladders. It was a way of building a house back then. Come on, your bath's waiting. We haven't got all night.'

Just water and a block of plain soap. No bubbles or bath salts, no perfume; nothing cloying, artificial. The low flicker of the candle. The quiet. Mel slips in behind her. A trickle of water down the curve of her back. Again, again, again. A chipped white enamel jug is constantly tipped, drowning out the cold. Afterwards she is towelled down. Patted between her legs, gentle, so gentle; encompassing. 'You need to heal,' he says, like a vet with a broken animal, 'grow everything back.'

'I know.'

'And fatten up, lass!' Feeling the wide wings of her too-defined hips. 'Give me some softness, some curves. Something to grip on to, girl.'

Connie laughs, remembering something Lara had said, how the best sex of her life had been when she'd put on weight, surrendered to her body and what it really wanted: 'A bit of chocolate, ice cream, enjoyment – a bit of flesh, my Connie girl! And lo and behold, he noticed me all over again. It sparked everything into life.'

Connie's hands range Mel's room in the golden light, wanting to seize it, every single bit of it, learn him, gouge him out. She takes up an ivory comb on its tray on the dressing table, a relic from another life, his mother's perhaps, and flicks Mel playfully around. 'Ssssh, your turn now, on the bed, quick.' She pushes him down and straddles him and ploughs his back with ivory that's the colour of shiny old bone, then his long arms, his thighs, the skittish soles of his feet. Reaping goosebumps. Swiftly he's enslaved.

'You now, madam,' Mel commands in response and Connie plunges her face into his pillow of simple stripes that's lumpy with age and uncaring; she collects his smell and breathes deep. Wanting all of it for ever, just this now, just this, for the world not to intrude on any of it.

'Your face is all light,' he says afterwards, running his finger down a cheek. 'Most people have shadows but with you, no, there's just this wonderful, clear light.'

'Now.'

'Yes.'

'Thanks to you.'

'Was it really so bad in the past?'

'It must have been. Yes, yes.'

35

Exposed on a high ledge in full light

A day of bellowing light. Giddied with it. Standing there, utterly naked in the yellow room ringing with its morning sun, utterly naked before Cliff's breakfast table. Tall with her newness, strong with it; vivid with life, exuberance, light. Pushing her locked hands above her head as if she is pushing the entire sky up, up.

'Have you gone quite mad?' Cliff enquires.

'Yes! Yes!'

'You seem very alive, all of a sudden. Perhaps we should take advantage of this.'

'No, no.' She flinches down.

'Where's your pretty little trinket?' He squints.

She's silent.

'Con? I need to see it.'

'Not now.'

'Play?'

'No.' She steps back.

A clotted silence.

'Is there anything you want?' Cliff asks carefully.

'I – I don't want to sponge or shave you any more.'

There, she's said it. A shardy quiet. Connie is emboldened.

'I think we should hire someone to do it. A woman. Someone. From the Philippines, Eastern Europe perhaps. Like a nurse. I don't mind.'

Cliff is quiet, taking it all in, everything that it means, this newness. A vein flinches in his temple. 'Right,' he says, slow.

'I'll hire her. I'll do it.'

'You have gone mad, haven't you?'

'Yes, yes!'

Connie stands before her husband, emblazoned, utterly bared, knowing that her path will now unfold like a flare shot from a gun, powering through the dark, and she just has to trust the brightness and its landfall wherever that will be. She is crashing catastrophe into her life, it has all begun. Her love for him has been snuffed, like a match extinguished, just like that it is gone and she knows it and she suspects he does too.

His knuckles tighten around his chair.

'Only you can do what you do. For me. For us.' The voice menacing, utterly careful, quiet. The bankers always win, always, Connie thinks in that moment, feeling like a great fist has squeezed her heart tight.

36

It rasped her, though, to have stirring about in her this brutal monster! to hear twigs cracking and feel hooves planted down in the depths of that leaf-encumbered forest, the soul

Discreet enquiries are made of the ladies who lunch.

Marichka comes into their world, she has to, Connie will not countenance the alternative now. A sturdy Ukrainian with a gold cross around her neck, shutting her off, and a fulsome, freckled face.

'I need a looker, I must have that. Couldn't bear to have to stare at something ugly all the time.'

Oh yes, Connie knows. She always serves Cliff well. Marichka has a boyfriend. He returned to Ukraine for the funeral of his grandmother and now can't get a working visa to return. He will, one day, but no one knows when. Perfect.

Cliff is resisting at first. Utterly stiff, dismissive, not seeing Marichka, really, who she actually is; he's like this with all the help. But gradually her brisk practicality softens him. She wins him with glasses of whisky whenever he seems to desire them, a sure, professional touch and endless games of poker she will play deep into the night and contentedly never win. Cliff gives up, surrenders his body to her and gradually lets her do what she wants. Lets her do everything for him, like a child, submits to her complete and calm benevolence.

Suddenly, just like that, he seems to be noticing his wife less and less. Not taking her hand now and holding it kindly, and he used at least to do that. Not noticing what she wears – the new skirt from Joseph, the maxi from Rellik – when he used to clock all of it and appreciate it. Not asking her to sit next to him at the breakfast table, none of it. She wonders what he has planned for her, what is next; wasn't expecting a silent withholding, doesn't trust it.

People create crises to speed up their evolution, Connie tells herself. Rupture is good for us, she tells herself. Even when you don't know what's next. She's sick of having her living deferred: you can't have a life of endlessly that. The hours ahead of all, all the hours in this house, closing over her like a steel trap.

Marichka watches over her. Brings her glasses of milk and chai tea lattes just when she needs them, tells her to go to bed, get some sleep. Entwining herself into both their lives.

37

But then anyone who's worth anything reads just what he likes, as the mood takes him, and with extravagant enthusiasm

'I want a relationship that's belly to belly not back to back. Isn't that a lovely expression? My Irish cleaner told it to me. It summed up her marriage, she said. Belly to belly.'

Mel does not answer. Does he want to get married again? No, not if it means the vast entanglement of a woman who turns into something else. His wife, still his wife, was so grandly neurotic, Machiavellian, complex, and she'd been none of that at the start. As punishment withheld sex. Her weapon. Mel is separated not divorced and has left all the connecting with people behind him for a good while, or thought he had; he is still shell-shocked. Belly to belly, what, he can't even think of how to answer that.

He looks at Connie, sitting exotically in the corner of his room, her silk-clad legs crossed and so utterly wrong in all this – like an orchid in a butcher's shop. No, not an orchid, she has the vulnerability of jasmine, yes that, so briefly blazing, heralding a softer, lovelier time before curling up. But would she wither like the rest of them? Trap him, then change? Where is the shrew in her, the nag? They all have that. Mel doesn't want to be broken again. Financially drained and harangued along with it. He's been like a dog licking its wounds for so long, called in now to the warmth. Yet he doesn't quite trust it. Look at Connie now, idly flitting her beautifully manicured nails along his books as if she can't quite believe his type would read, let alone all this; surely it's wall-to-wall football, the *Sun* and endless *Corrie* with his lot.

So many books on bowed bookshelves, hardbacks stripped of their jackets, paperbacks almost oily with the reading and rereading. Connie thinks of the grand rise of bookshelves at home. They hired a professional book buyer to stock the shelves, to convey the image of exquisite taste. Her side of the fireplace: Booker winners, literary fiction, a lot from India; his: histories, biography, the odd frivolity about carp or the genesis of fat. Handsome hardbacks, first editions, often signed, some rarities but Connie can't remember what. She wasn't allowed to slip in her own scuffed paperbacks, all her dog-eared women, her passions from youth, her secret pillow books. Here, in this humbly neat little room Camus and Hardy jostle with Kafka and James; other worlds, other lives. Amis senior, Joyce, McEwan, Le Carré, Rushdie, McCarthy, Doyle and a shock of women. Mansfield. Austen. Byatt. O'Brien. Woolf, goodness, so much of that. Connie slips out *To the Lighthouse* and opens it. *NEVER READ THIS AGAIN*, shouts stern ink in horror, right across the frontispiece, from some unknown reader. She whoops a laugh. Holds up the page.

'I found it at an Oxfam in Bath. Couldn't resist it with a message like that. Just had to read it. It's the naughty little boy in me. Always doing what I'm told not to.'

'But why Woolf? And there's so much of her.'

Mel shrugs. 'I read anything. She tells me what women think. She tells me the truth. It's so hard to get it out of you lot. Have *you* read her?'

'No.'

'You should. All women should.'

Lara has said that to her too. Connie makes a mental note. 'Belly to belly, don't you love that?' she tries again, nudging the book back then changing her mind and slipping it into her jacket pocket.

Mel looks at her. The way she just filched his book, without asking, that princessy sense of entitlement. Connie looks down on him, of course; he's her amusement, diversion, a bit of rough. An uneducated, working-class white boy: the most maligned and disadvantaged of the lot. From Stoke, a northern city that the steelworks and coalmines clothed triumphantly in a sooty black; the grime throughout his childhood settled on everything: windows, washing, his mother's face, his father's lungs. He went to a bog-standard comprehensive and didn't even finish it; Connie went independent, a West Country boarding school, it's in her voice and her grace. She followed it with a respectable second in English Lit and he's not even sure what that means, has never got his head around the way unis work along with those secret codes of pronunciation – Cholmondeley, Cadogan, Magdalen, Fettes – that all of them seem to know about, shutting out the rest and he always has to ask, embarrassing himself. It infuriates him that in this country, still, your prospects in life are determined by birth; such a vicious, Third World form of inequality. It festers, just to think about it. What would Connie Carven know about the mystery of powerlessness? If you've not been raised in disadvantage how could you possibly understand?

'Did you know that richer, thicker kids will always end up getting further ahead in these parts than brighter, poorer kids?'

'Sorry?'

Connie shakes her head, scrabbling with where Mel's coming from. Is it a slight . . . an insult . . . on her . . . Cliff? Surely not. She feels like a swimmer suddenly caught in a soft, insistent rip.

'What are you saying?'

Mel sighs, says nothing more, it's no use trying to explain to the likes of her what enrages him about this garden and its shareholders and their gilded offspring in their grey and red coats. He sees it, hears it all the time from those not a part of this oblivious set. What would she know of the poison of envy? He has a young stepdaughter and how it used to rile his wife – that her child was destined for the local primary, her life marked out from that point and it would take an extraordinary spirit in someone so young to haul themselves above it. Nowhere in Notting Hill can Mel see the bracing rigour of a meritocracy. The hugely expensive nursery nearby – where Connie's son would surely be sent – is a feeder for Prince William's old pre-prep which is a conveyor belt into feeders for Eton and Westminster which are well-worn paths to Oxbridge and the upper echelons of British politics. So. The shaping of the nation's elite begins at three. Of course.

Does Connie get that? Could she possibly? That glittery prospects are bought? Does she notice it, care? He thinks not. UK politicians are being drawn from an increasingly narrow pool, of course, yet what would she care; right now the Prime Minister, his deputy and Chancellor all went to schools with fees substantially higher than Mel's wage. The bruise of inequality enrages Mel, the stain on this world no matter how bright you are. Connie, poor lost soul that she is, would have no idea of the depth of the rage around her, the infuriating sense of impotence, and there's no use trying to explain it.

She looks at Mel now, sitting in his armchair, so knotted all of a sudden, so sullen and uncommunicative. Her eyes narrow like a cat's. She feels so very apart from him tonight, vexingly, like they're standing on opposite river banks with a rush of water roaring between them and can't hear each other, will never be able to hear each other. How can this possibly work? She stands, chest tight. This is ridiculous. The gulf too great. Leaves with scarcely a goodbye, the book still in her pocket.

Which Mel notes.

38

We do not know our own souls, let alone the souls of others. Human beings do not go hand in hand the whole stretch of the way. There is a virgin forest in each; a snowfield where even the print of birds' feet is unknown. Here we go alone, and like it better so. Always to have sympathy, always to be accompanied, always to be understood would be intolerable

Shopping is Connie's drug. She has to control its dosage and then the urge overtakes her and if she sees something she must have, but it is not in her size, she will rise magnificent and track it down with the thoroughness of a detective on the scent. The sweetness of a purchase, the vast sweetness; within the tumult of loveliness that is Notting Hill, Marylebone, Bond Street, Westfield Shepherd's Bush. She'll do High Street as much as high end, she'll do anything. Her walk-in wardrobe brims, she forgets what she has and often ends up wearing the same favoured thing, day after day. No matter. Her appetite has her wolfishly prowling not just shops for fresh stock but websites. Interrupted by Cliff e-mailing obscene photos of women being penetrated by men with enormous cocks, often black, begging her teasingly for 'play', informing her it's 'what she really wants', reeling her in. She looks, still looks, shuts her eyes on it.

Shopping, for Connie, is a deeply alone pursuit. She could not bear for anyone else to witness her greed, her thrill, her sharkish intent. Spying something she likes, she'll often linger slow by something else, as if to gather herself, calm her heartbeat, for the thrill of the kill. Alone she will secrete the bags home, alone tumble the purchases upon her bed, alone dress up for another

viewing then disperse into the cupboards and drawers,
forget . . .

She always looks effortless. It takes hours to perfect.
 Mel would be revolted, by all of it.

39

To love makes one solitary

Connie has not been into the garden for days and days and then with a rush she is there, in an afternoon of roaring light and air that is thinning with a coming summer; she can no longer hold herself back. She hears the catch of his pale breath as she comes upon him. Under her thin coat of red dots she is naked but for silken black panties, a wisp of them.

'It's too early . . .' – he backs back – 'people are about.'

'I don't care.' She is flinging aside his shovel and hauling him into the shed, the neck of his T-shirt in her hungry fist. 'I do. not. care. All right?'

'All right.' Laughing, giving in.

He is pleased to see her, so pleased, it is a deepening; this lively little sprig of jasmine is vining his life; taking over his calm, his thoughts, his retreat into solitude, his flinty remoteness. Quick, his hands break the band of her thong and push it aside, quick, his fingers slip into both holes, bringing Connie to pleasure with a sure touch, oiling her up until she collapses in on herself, again, and again, and again, and then he encircles her trembling and just holds, and holds, his hand protective over her secret places. A still quiet. No talk, of course, never that straight afterwards, he knows she does not want the crash of that, is learning her fast.

Her flinching quietens. 'Thank you for coming back,' he whispers finally, hoarse.

Connie just lies there, encircled by him, and the tears slowly run from her eyes. Crying, snotting, all phlegm and fluid; for she is loosened, completely, released. Mel does nothing, just wraps her in the encompassing peace of his body. All is still, humble, quiet. It is the stillness of a man found, as he holds her, he knows it. No matter how much he tries to resist.

The passion for him moves in Connie's belly once again, she resists it as far as she can, must get back, Cliff is at home this evening, she can't. But quick. She stirs him and he responds, his touch so much more competitive and creative than Cliff's has ever been. There is no complacency, no taking for granted, he wants his stroking, licking, caressing, cherishing to be remembered. It's as if he wants to wipe all her husband's ways like a whiteboard freshened; to stamp her skin with the permanence of his own stroke. He flips her, wants something else. Her buttocks spread wide, a cool breath, a nudging, a trembling, a reticence, into her arse, gently, probing, so careful not to hurt.

'Ow,' she gasps, and he withdraws: 'Another time.'

'No, no, now.'

He is on her, moving – surely the thrusting of pale buttocks is a little ridiculous, Connie is thinking, how silly they must look, to anyone who came upon them – then a finger is in her vagina, the skin between the two passages is so thin, paper thin and so sensitively he works until her body takes over, surrenders to the exquisiteness and she comes; they both do, together. And fall back and laugh.

'I've never done that before. Come, at the same time with someone. Ever.'

'Most people haven't.'

'You know, more than a few women I know have never come.'

'Really? Even now . . . in this day and age.' Mel shakes his head.

'Oh yes. Or they haven't come until their late thirties or forties at least. Not that you men ever know these things.'

'You came. I can tell. I always can.'

'Yes.' And for a while there she thought she'd never be able to again, in the thick of Cliff, without all the help. She smiles. There is only one word for how Connie feels now, in the sanctity of this quiet.

Anchored.

40

*I want someone to sit beside after the day's
pursuit and all its anguish, after its listening, its
waitings, and its suspicions. After quarrelling and
reconciliation I need privacy – to be alone with
you, to set this hubbub in order. For I am as
neat as a cat in my habits*

It is late, they cannot part; Cliff will be home now, they must. Connie feels the terrible weight of Mel and tries to extract herself, can't; he is stroking her, cupping her between her legs, playful; the hair has almost grown back. 'Ah my lovely, lovely – healthy – cunt of a thing.'

'What!' She bats him away, laughing. 'That *word*. Excuse me. It's appalling. I can't believe you just said it. The only men who ever say it are men who don't like women very much.'

'Cunt cunt cunt,' he is teasing, relishing it on the tongue. 'I love saying it. All of it.'

'Excuse me,' Connie admonishes. 'A woman is trained to distrust the man – and the circumstance – whenever we hear it. To castigate and protest.'

'Cunt cunt, lovely cunt.' Mel buries his head into her. 'For me it's entirely something else. It's you, it's this, it's sex, it's inside you, outside you, it's the whole damned loveliness, the whole blinking lot. Let me . . . change . . . the word for you.' He stops, thinks. 'It's a precious thing. Something to revel in, cherish. It's not just fucking. Argh, I can do that with anyone and bollocks to it. But this, *this*, wakes me up. Hauls me into . . .' He struggles for the word.

'What?'

'The world again. And I'd given up on it, until a little

bird came into my life.' Mel looks at Connie – 'Yes' – with his warm, kind, speaking eyes. She kisses him softly, rightly between them, in chuff. 'It really has,' he adds.

'I know,' she whispers, kissing his thick black lashes that still have something of the little boy in them, first one side, now the other, in rhythmic gentleness. 'Do you care for me? Do you? Really?'

'What do you think? I try my hardest to resist you – everything you represent – but can't. Just . . . can't.'

Mel's hands curve firm over Connie's body not with desire now but a cherishing, an ownership. A pleasure that all is well, and all is his, *his*, as if he can scarcely believe it. He kisses her with the lifetime's tenderness in it and Connie marvels at that – when Cliff had not a scrap.

'Thank you,' Connie whispers, 'thank you.'

The day is winding down and she runs home through air that is vibrant with stillness. What has happened, what has transpired on this day feels like an anointing, a hauling into womanhood, finally, a strong, rooted maturing into something else – or at least a journey's departing. Connie runs home to the hull of her marriage, high and dry on its sand. The kiss with all the world's tenderness singing through her still, giddying her up. The touch of his lips, like voice, something she will never forget. She just knows it.

Connie's heart like an oven, a furnace, just opened. The heat of it, the roar. She cannot slam it shut. Who can tell? Everyone? The blare of it.

She rushes in to the kitchen. Marichka is spoon-feeding Cliff ice cream, the last of it and Connie has no idea why but he is lapping it up. Some game they are playing. She comes upon them like an intrusion. It is a scene of collusion, tinged in early evening light, a sixteenth-century Dutch painting of domesticity, caring, quiet. Marichka looks up at her like, so, whatever works. Connie nods, yes, whatever works, keep on going, girl, keep at it. But there is something new in her stance, a freshness, a wildness, Marishka can sense it in the other woman. She slips away. Connie turns and watches her depart, wondering for a moment if she is listening by the door.

Steps forward. Takes a deep breath.

'Clifford' – she only calls her husband this when something serious is to be said – 'would you like me to have a baby one day?'

From her husband: furtive apprehension. Trying to second-guess what comes next. To control, to win, command, as he always wins.

'I wouldn't mind,' he says carefully. A pause. 'As long as it made no difference between us.'

41

With her foot on the threshold she waited a moment longer in a scene which was vanishing even as she looked, and then, as she moved . . . and left the room, it changed, it shaped itself differently; it had become, she knew, giving one last look at it over her shoulder, already the past

Connie cocks her head.

'Yes. I could be quite willing, I suppose, as long as it doesn't affect our marriage.' He's like a cornered dog, thinking aloud, trying to see ahead, work it through. 'Affect what we have. Con.' The voice lowering, warning. 'Nothing must come between us. Why are you saying this? What's going on?' He is suddenly cold, brittle, as still as a hoary January frost. Connie recognizes it. It is a threat. Cliff crushes people, of course; that's how he's always succeeded, in his business and his life. Rivals, colleagues, friends, clients.

Leaving him – magnificent rupture – would humiliate him, of course, the anger would be encompassing and immense. Connie is inside the black oil of his mind now, inside his desire to infiltrate, dominate, swamp. She is all Cliff has. All he wants is for her to stay with him, in this, the husk of his life; be with him for ever, propping him up, his sexual regenerator and adornment. He needs the public show of that, the public theatre of his power over this aspect of his life. This man before her is almost an emotional cripple – and she does not know how she can extricate herself.

'A child would seem just like my own, I guess. If it's done right. Legally. Emotionally. People will ask. We'd keep things to ourselves, of course. I'd get everything water-tight. Contracts and so forth.' He's talking it through, trying to make it work. Connie is listening, her heart breaking. He is willing to do this – something he categorically does not want – for their marriage. To keep up the pretence, to have her by his side, to preserve the past in aspic. He is taking over this too as he takes over everything and he doesn't even realize it; his unbending way with control. No, it could never work. For her or a child, and Cliff doesn't understand and most likely never would. Connie has wondered if he'd ever fall in love with Marichka – if the hired help could be her distraction, her saviour – but she's a diversion, nothing more than that. She sees it now. He would never publicly be with her, he wouldn't stoop. There's no cachet in the hired help. As for Connie . . .

'Come here,' he commands. 'Kiss me.'

As if he senses something new in his wife, something quite incomprehensible and he needs to sniff it out. Some straightness of the spine, a looseness, a stepping back.

'Kiss me!' he demands.

Connie hackles at the thought: the stumpy, joyless, wooden blocks of his mouth. He revolts her, with every hair of her body, she can't do it, can't explain it.

'No, Cliff, not tonight.'

'Why?' Wounded.

'I just don't want to. I'm tired.'

Connie turns, murmurs goodbye, cannot meet her husband's eyes. Cannot tell him she is not coming near him because another man's smell and his sperm is strong upon her, smeared lavishly and triumphantly across her stomach, breasts, thighs; and she is rank, filthy with it and cannot hurt him so much.

'Con? Con!' The voice bewildered suddenly, on the cusp of an understanding, as if Cliff has suddenly caught a glimpse of a future he has never contemplated.

She does not turn back. Mustn't.

42

My own brain is to me the most unaccountable of machinery – always buzzing, humming, soaring roaring diving, and then buried in mud. And why? What's this passion for?

A restless mongrel of a night, spatterings of rain like hard rice against the high windows. The wind wheening outside Connie's room is as mournful as a distant aria and the trees from the garden below shake their leaves like the manes of recalcitrant ponies and wet leaves slick the glass. Connie will not bath, wants to keep the animal smell on her, of earth, of sex, of spit and air and grubbiness. She will not wash herself all night, for the sense of Mel's flesh touching her, his very stickiness, is dear, replenishing, holy. She no longer wants padlocks and blindfolds, sophistication, theatre, clandestine texts, she just wants simplicity. The wonder of that. One man, who listens. Stillness. Spirituality. Quiet. Her cunt reeks, she wants wildness, wants to roll herself in it, wants a different soil, sky, land to this. Wordsworth journeyed back to Wales to listen to the language of his former heart; should she return to Cornwall? With Mel? Go somewhere else? Would he come? What to do, how to begin . . . what?

Connie's mind is jumpy tonight with dreams and plans and connivances and plots as she contemplates a vast spring cleaning of her future, her entire life. Her gods now – the gods of change and rupture and the astonishing earth.

Connie looks across at her bookshelf, an old shoe rack

from the Golborne Road, and skims all the strong female voices that have spined her own life. Any clues? Help? Are all female narratives of empowerment narratives of escape? It's why *Portrait of a Lady* is so devastating, of course, why she could only ever bear to read it once. She picks up Mel's battered old Virginia Woolf. *NEVER READ THIS AGAIN* – but of course, no, she must. 'I'm always doing what I'm told not to,' that's what he said to her that odd, jangly night. Connie thinks of his separateness, his self-containment, the potency of a man strong with his choices and not wavering from them. She flips open *To the Lighthouse* and starts to read. The thud of recognition, the heart-stopping thud of it, and she scrabbles for a journal and scribbles in it. Again and again. A roar of pages filled up.

> *A sort of transaction went on between them, in which she was on one side, and life was on another, and she was always trying to get the better of it, as it was of her.*

Yes, yes. Woolf will be her guide, her beacon. All her novels, her essays, her certainties and admonishments and eviscerating truths. Tomorrow she will go to Daunt's, buy the extent of her.

She must act. Just that. Now, before it is too late.

43

There is no doubt in my mind, that I have found out how to begin to say something in my own voice

The intercom, buzzing in her bedroom. Insistent. Connie picks it up. Neither greeting nor warmth. 'Prepare yourself. You have an hour. I'll be in my office.'

The voice struts. Ah, the Cliff of old.

Connie's hand reaches down, she is a different woman now, she has been hauled into a different life and her body blazes it. She is fuller and softer and looser, hairier; her body less brittle, self-hating, desperate. No, she will do this, reveal herself. It is the start of the new life and Cliff must know it. She stands proud in front of the mirror, marvelling at the fresh self. Reclaimed, returned to nature, the earth.

The intercom again. 'Bring your trinket. I want to put it in. I want to snap it shut.'

Connie does not respond, cannot. The punctures would be closed up now, surely, faint scars all that's left of her former life. The padlock lies somewhere lost in the dirt near the shed, claimed by the undergrowth. She mustn't think how much it was worth.

Connie turns back the mirror, biting her lip; back to her new body and everything it signals about her release. Her husband waits. She will not shave herself, she will not give him what he wants; the fury will be incandescent. Connie is very still, for a moment, stuck. What is she doing? What will be the consequences? Is she mad?

She suddenly feels like she's standing barefoot on oysters, stranded by an incoming tide, can't move but can't stay, stuck.

She must go down.

Cannot be a fugitive in her own house. She showers, throws on the silken kimono, ties it languidly, ready for a slipping off. Pads slowly down, down the grand staircase, breathing measured and calm, collecting herself.

Shuts the office door behind her. The screen is down; it runs almost the length of one wall. So, a video, porn, right; and usually as she watches them with Cliff the liquid warmth plumes through her despite herself and she cannot help but succumb, despite herself, widening her legs on her chair and playing as Cliff hands across a vibrator, and another, as he toys with his Mont Blanc pen, the secret signal that begins it all and she is opening out, needing the coming, urgently, the next step. And she is greedy with the looking at these films as long as it doesn't veer into anything too long, or monotonous; it is all the thrill, the anticipation that she wants.

Cliff wheels up to her now, vividness in his face, a video camera in his lap; he has sometimes filmed in the past and she has played up to it, trusting, yielding so much; entranced. 'I need my wife back.'

Eagerly his Mont Blanc pen tugs the bow of her kimono, loosens it. The silk falls open. Connie drops the gown from her shoulders. Her husband gasps. It is as if a vast gulf suddenly separates them. As if his wife has gone on a strange new journey without him knowing anything of it. He has not controlled it in any way, has not allowed it, she is lost.

'It – it doesn't mean anything to me any more, Cliff.

It's just . . . gone.' She shrugs. 'Everything we do. All of it.' She shuts her eyes on hot wet. 'I'm so sorry.'

They stare at each other, the two of them who have bared so much, gone on such a journey in tandem, nothing to say because there is nothing to say. The whole scenario worked because it was the two of them together, in an entranced and astonished collaboration. Cliff's lips tighten. He spins his chair. 'I wish you'd told me,' he says, tight. He clicks on the film, a black man with an enormous cock and a white woman with impossible breasts, the ridiculous thrusting, the ugly close-up, the monotony, the bleakness, the utter absence of mystery and beauty in any of it; Connie cannot watch.

She picks up her robe, puts it back on and ties the belt firm and tight.

'I'm so sorry.'

A match snuffed.

'I need something else now.'

'What?' The word is spat, as if Cliff can hardly bear to ask.

Connie shrugs, helpless. 'Life.'

Cliff's face. Pale with fury and devastation and loss.

44

To be silent; to be alone. All the being and the doing, expansive, glittering, vocal, evaporated; and one shrunk, with a sense of solemnity, to being oneself

Sunday morning. Needing a quietening. A necessary removal from all of them, to recalibrate. What is happening to Connie as uncertainty and indecision stain her life? A drawing to . . . what? Mystery. A veering towards it like an ocean liner subtly altering course for a new destination in the great ocean of life. Yet the destination's unknown.

Before Cliff's accident Connie had attended church. He certainly didn't, ever, still doesn't; one of those pitbull atheists, a sneerer à la Dawkins. Yet increasingly she's finding there's something . . . all-calming . . . about her Sunday morning experiences at the family-crammed church of St Peter's in its high, shouting ochre on Notting's hill. It's an astonishing leak through a veneer of aspirant coolness and moneyed cynicism; a gentle drip, drip, through her restless, caged, unsettled life. Connie feels righted by these assignations, balmed, lit.

'I like that you go to church,' Mel said to her once, even though he doesn't go himself. As if it softens her. As if it separates her from those who are the jeering, the sneering, the unsettled – and the ones with a chip of ice.

So. Sunday mornings, quite bravely alone. Connie's brief coracle of solace. Brought down into stillness by a spiritual enveloping from a service mostly sung. The hour or so freshening, shining, rejuvenating. At times she says no, it's ridiculous, she's with that gentle atheist, Alain de Botton on this one; tipping her hat to the graces within organized religion but not sucked in by them. Yet Connie knows that she'll never be aligned with the Cliffs and the Dawkins of the world, thumping that believers are deluded, stupid; she has too much respect for the mysterious in life. Which includes Mel. Can't turn her back on wonder, craves it, in a sense. Found it, long ago, in the wild places of her travelling youth, the places where the silence hums – Greenland's ice deserts, Cornwall's high moors, under a full butter moon – yes, yes. She wants those places again. Somewhere in her life. Her rescue is tied up in them, she just knows it.

Connie feels silted up, often now, with the great weight of acquiring and cramming and rushing and worrying and just getting by; grubbied. Needs the simplicity of a spiritual way, its light touch, a tuning fork back into calm. The ocean liner on its unknown path is veering her towards those most shining qualities of religious practice: pilgrimage, contemplation, quiet. With Mel, she hopes. Somehow.

What she does know: that religion's a miracle of survival. That places of potent spirituality do not belong entirely to earth. The tugging, the faint whisper of a tugging . . . and Connie has to find her way back to them. Urgently, it feels now.

Alone, or with someone else.

45

I want to think quietly, calmly, spaciously, never to be interrupted, never to have to rise from my chair, to slip easily from one thing to another, without any sense of hostility, or obstacle. I want to sink deeper and deeper, away from the surface, with its hard separate facts

Everywhere the lovely tight buds of the roses, waiting for a springing into bloom, everywhere the vast loosening as light floods weary, winter-bowed bones, everywhere an uncurling, an unfolding. People, their faces open to the sky, flowers, the happy philadelphus and yellow-wort and the springing grass before the dryness of summer and it all turns to leaching heat and spareness and dust; it's a tingling day of high giddiness and Connie wants to grab all of it, all, this teeming exuberance, wander through it with eyes wide and fingers trailing and be replenished, by all of it, smell it and giggle and delight. In the garden, of course.

'I want to touch you like you touch me,' she tells Mel. 'I've never really touched your body, properly, like you have mine.'

'How do I touch you?'

'With reverence. I'll never forget it. Because no man's ever touched me like that before. If I never saw you again, after this day, I'd remember your touch for the rest of my life. It's . . . stamped. Yes, that's the word. Stamped. By tenderness. I'll never forget it.'

Connie straddles Mel's supine body and shuts her eyes and places her two palms flat on his chest.

'You feel me as if you're blind. As if it's the last time you'll ever touch me, every time you do that. It's like you're committing everything to memory, wondering and delighting and . . . sanctifying . . . yes, that. So I'll never forget you. It's a gift, you know.'

Mel's penis stirs under her hand, Connie slips it into her, moves on him, soft. Brings him into a coming with her sensitivity learned and her quietness and as he peaks she bears down on him, voluptuous and feels him spasming in her like a dying animal and embraces as if it's the last time, the last time ever, and she will never forget.

'Do you know what you're doing?' he pants. 'You're trapping me.'

'Yes, ssssh, it's all right, no talk.' A fingertip brushes down Mel's lips, a vast smile fills her up.

46

They came to her, naturally, since she was a woman,
all day long with this and that; one wanting this,
another that; the children were growing up; she
often felt she was nothing but a sponge sopped full
of human emotions

On a glary morning of high heat Connie feels a quickening in her womb, as if the sunshine has touched it
and bloomed it into happiness. All about her, nannies
and babies in the garden and chitter-chat, all about her,
friends falling pregnant, baby showers, girlfriends
needing coffees and catch-ups and movie nights. Connie's
always a good sounding board, someone peaceful and
repairing to have about. They call her a lot, checking
up. She's a listener, a deep pool of stillness and quiet
just waiting to receive, one of those rare ones who never
wants to talk about herself. She doesn't butt in over
sentences, trying to dazzle with her own thoughts,
doesn't crash into conversations with ever bigger and
better and more hilarious anecdotes.

Connie wonders, though, at yet another brasserie of
blonde wood and ringing talk, if the social world is
becoming a little more shouty now, raucous, in your
face? Everyone's so eager to talk at you, over the top
of you, cram in their two bobs' worth – but actually,
quietly, to enquire? To listen deeply? No, she doesn't
see much of that. Only with Mel, who asks so many
questions of her and it's so odd in a man; he seems at
times as if he wanted to drink her up. Needing to
understand.

She longs often for Mel's quiet. The comfort of their

silence, in sync. With Cliff the silence was oppressive, accusatory, as it shouted their differences, that they had so little in common and how did they get to this and they must spend the rest of their lives amid it.

Connie's book club is fracturing as hospital appointments, pregnancy yoga classes, exhaustion, end-of-year concerts and summer parties disrupt life. Again and again it feels like Connie's friends are succumbing and falling pregnant but they're always careful with this news around her, Cliff being Cliff of course, and the accident . . . and she's always so reticent about that side of her life now, poor lamb . . . there's been a vast reassessing, a reining back . . . it must be very painful, not too much is asked.

'Tragic, all of it. Such a supreme alpha male. He probably couldn't bear the thought of anyone else's child so that's that, I guess. She's the good wife, Con. Bless.'

No, Connie would not be drawn. On any of it. Such a rare orchid in her exquisitely tasteful, lonely married life; pitied, talked about, endlessly called on to be godmother as if that would be enough. But her thinking veers so fundamentally, often now; she's reluctant to bring a child into this jangly, jittery world of keeping up, couldn't say any of this to any of them. Sees it again and again, all around her: how children seem to send the women around her slightly mad. Piteously obsessed. Is it exhaustion? Empowerment now they're no longer at work? Competitive banker husbands demanding too much of everyone? Too much time on their hands?

The friends who turn into harridans, bullies, where their child's school is involved, haranguing the teachers and the principals over their precious, infinitely talented darlings; demanding better results, more readings in church, a bigger role in the school play, more tuition, attention, certificates. Imogen has a poo phobia so can never change her baby's nappies, has to have round-the-clock help and Connie wonders if it's a secret canniness. Charlotte, Honor and Floss have weekend nannies alongside nannies for each child during the week; when, Connie wonders, are those children actually noticed, let alone surrounded by their parents, basted in love like butter and cherished? India endlessly rails over the mobile phones given out as party gifts at a girl's twelfth birthday, yet gives out goldfish to every child at her son's sixth. Then the flurry of end-of-year teacher presents: the voluptuous bouquets from Wild at Heart as big as a television, bottles of Moët, exquisite gift boxes from Space NK. Then there's the horror of the entrance exams, when her friends disappear into an insanity of pushing and tutoring and hating and shouting and deep, wrenching torment over who got into what. For Connie, sitting back among it all and quietly listening, endlessly listening, this world feels mad, unhinged, overripe.

Could she ever raise a child amid all this?

With no money, at that?

Could she ever compete on the back foot – or would she go mad with it?

47

I have been stained by you and corrupted . . .
What dissolution of the soul you demanded in
order to get through one day, what lies, bowings,
scrapings, fluency and servility! How you chained
me to one spot, one hour, one chair, and sat
yourself down opposite! How you snatched from
me the white spaces that lie between hour and
hour and rolled them into dirty pellets and
tossed them into the wastepaper basket with
your greasy paws. Yet those were my life.

Summer is unfurling like a carpet Connie steps upon. Out, out, she must be out in it, often, away from the prison of her house. Its thickness of atmosphere. Cliff is biding his time, she can tell; the punishment is brewing and it will be magnificent. She does not know what correcting will befall her since that day when she boldly bared her new self to him, when she finally said no, enough. Cliff has been icily civil ever since but she knows it's not the end of it; there are little pinpricks of put-downs, often now, leaking through his veneer of control. Once they would have eaten away at Connie but no, not now, because she has something else: an anchor in another life.

'You could never get a job, Con, you've been out of the workforce too long. No one would have you. And you'd do . . . what?' '*Another* bag from Rellik? Do you need help? Shoppers Anonymous perhaps?' 'Are you getting fat?' 'Is that a tummy I can spy coming along?' Yet still Cliff does not know of Mel, Connie is sure of it, it is just a sense of . . . difference . . . a chasm opening up that he can almost sniff out. And so the attempts at shattering her confidence, reining her back, before it is too late.

Even when they are together, even when there is the pretence of that, Connie is not with him now. On this, a trilling day of sprightly light, she cannot resist. Cliff is in his chair by the bench on the lawn and she is expected in her place, her papers on her lap, their public ritual of solidity and togetherness that is noted by everyone who strolls the park. But Connie can't help it. As Cliff is buried in the *How to Spend It* magazine she slips into the lip of her wild place. Knows she should not. The risk, the risk.

Mel comes up the path from the shed, is able to cup her breast quick and lift it in enquiry and smile secrets then, 'Con, Con!' comes Cliff's voice from the lawn. Mel grimaces, she departs.

Cliff has a new wheelchair. It's just been shipped across from the States. Custom-built, state-of-the-art, designed by Philippe Starck, a slip of a thing of enormous strength. He is testing it out, wants Connie to see it. He has moved across to grass that needs a cutting, is trying to get up the soft slope and determined to do it as if attempting to haul himself into independence, movement, action and this new contraption will be the grand symbol of it. The chair struggles with its grip, with the weight. 'Come on, you little beauty!' he admonishes. 'You can do it.' It goes slowly. Connie is now beside him, encouraging him, softly.

They stop for a breather by a large oak. A squirrel races up the trunk and looks at them quizzically from a high branch. 'Look!' Connie cries out. 'It approves, Cliff, it's laughing at us.'

'Fucking vermin,' Cliff snaps. 'They should all be trapped and burnt. I'd get the gardener to do it – and watch.'

'Oh.' The charming side of her husband that no one but Connie ever sees.

They push on, the chair climbing slowly in its unwilling way. The earth is yielding to it too much, clogging up its wheels. The chair suddenly stops.

'Blast this wretched thing.'

'Let me push.'

'No,' Cliff says coldly. 'I didn't buy it for that.'

Connie tries, can't help it.

'Get the fuck *off* it.'

All the anger in him, from the other day, in his office, all the anger from the past twelve months. Without a word Connie tries to shove the contraption clear, to get him started again. It's surprisingly hard. Cliff hits back at her with all his might, hits her away from his chair, away from his life. 'You are pathetic, useless. You can't even listen, can you, you fucking cunt?'

Connie is very, very calm. 'I saw the gardener over there.' Her voice is neutral, her face tight. 'In the trees. The wild bit. Perhaps he can help.'

'Well, go and fucking well get him.'

Cliff hits the wheels in frustration. At himself, his wife, his spectacle of a life. 'If only I could get out and have a look at this fucking cunt of a thing myself.'

Connie strides off and shouts into the trees, 'Hello? Mel? Can you come and help us, please?' Not a trace of anything in her voice.

Obediently he comes, shovel loose in hand. Face blank, she business-like. 'Do you know anything about wheelchairs?'

'No.'

'Could you just see if anything's stuck in the wheels, or broken perhaps?'

Mel drops the shovel. Leans down on the ground.

Connie catches a glimpse of his back where his T-shirt rides up, the stretch of golden skin. Her thighs clench.

'Get your hands in there, come on, man, is there anything underneath, anything caught?' Cliff's voice utterly superior, admonishing, cold. 'You're not afraid of a bit of muck, are you?'

'No, sir.'

Mel lies flat on his stomach, trying to work out the mechanism underneath, tinkering, poking, prodding. His hands, shorts, are soon streaked with grass stains and black. But he's done something right. The motor coughs, splutters into life.

'I'll need some help.'

Mel looks directly at her, into her, grins a secret grin. Cliff doesn't catch it. And before he can protest Connie is behind the chair, firm against Mel, they are pushing in tandem, muscle against muscle, sinew against sinew, locked together and complicit and triumphant. It's hard work. The slope is punishing, the machine coughing and protesting.

'Leave me alone!' Cliff snaps. 'I can do it now.'

Immediately they fall back and watch, shoulder to shoulder. Immediately the chair looks vulnerable, it veers off, starts to tip and Mel rushes up and catches it just in time. No thanks from Cliff, just an exasperated sigh as once again he struggles with the buttons and knobs; the alpha man from the alpha world, humiliated. Turning it on and off, trying to churn it forward with a sheer raging will that is impotent. 'You'll rip her insides out if you keep doing that,' Mel remarks softly.

'Oh, fuck off.'

The chair firms again and lurches off the grass, rumbles across the gravel.

'You see, she's doing it!'

Then he catches Mel's face behind him. 'Are you helping it? Are you?'

'It won't do it by itself, sir. It's shot.'

'Fuck *off*. I've just paid a hell of a lot of money for this.'

Without another word the gardener picks up his shovel and strides off. The chair stops immediately, there's a sickening grate of knobs, nothing works.

'Mel? Mel!' Cliff barks.

The gardener strides to him. Without a word drops to the ground. Is on his back now, tinkering with something else. 'Start it up,' he commands finally, in an utterly dead voice Connie has never heard before. It works, half-hearted, with Mel and Connie's help pushing. A whirring, across the gravel at last, both machine and man tackling the job and punishingly hard work for the lot of them. Then the chair stops as if that's it, for good.

'Well, it's obvious I'm at everyone's fucking mercy.'

Jagged silence.

'You'll have to get back into the house, Clifford,' Connie says.

'Well?' He looks at Mel. 'Can you bear it?'

His superior tone. His coldness. A question and a command. Mel is expressionless. Without another word he hauls up the huge bulk of Clifford in a fireman's lift and carries him into the house in utter silence. Connie looks at the strange intimacy of it; her husband silent, humiliated, her lover's face white with effort for Cliff is a big man, six foot four. Mel's hands are trembling towards the end with the vast strain of it. Connie can't bear it. 'Over there, quick, that armchair by the door,' and Cliff is dumped into it as if Mel can't do this a step longer. He is paler than Connie has ever seen him, and remote, absent. He stands back, quiet, waiting for whatever is next.

His frailness, against the big bulk of her husband. His grace, his litheness, his vulnerability. Connie stares at him as if she has never seen it before. The straining muscles, every one of them put to work; the beauty of him within the thick of hard labour. The civil stoicism amid such astonishing incivility. The determination not to give up. It makes Connie want to rush up to Mel, hold him; she cannot. All her soul goes out to him and he is so silent, removed, out of reach in her house, in front of her husband, in this vast shell of a place. So utterly lost to her in this moment as he waits for something, anything, an apology, a thank you.

Nothing comes.

Of course. 'Thank you, thank you so much,' Connie gushes to him while Clifford is scrabbling to arrange himself, scrabbling out his mobile phone, stabbing the number of the wheelchair company to roar his complaint and focused entirely on that, on himself.

'I'll see you out,' Connie says quietly and by the door lifts Mel's trembling hand, once, in a courtly gesture of a kiss. Drops it swift. 'I'm sorry,' she whispers and he smiles his thanks, deep into her, smiles his understanding at last as Cliff shouts oblivious down his phone. They feel so together, in that moment, more than they ever have before, united against this man and this world and then Mel is gone back, back, to his work.

Connie had once dreamed of a friendship between these two men, a child raised together, an odd threesome full of secrets but something that worked. She knows now it could never be; neither man would countenance it. Oil and water, their hostility instinctive and immense. Neither respects the other.

Connie hates Cliff. Yes, hates him, from this afternoon, she has suddenly realized it. The depth of her feeling has not taken shape until this incident and what a freeing thing it is, exhilarating, enervating, to finally admit it to herself. There is no guilt. Now I hate him I shall never be able to go on living with him, she thinks. He's a dead fish of a man, dead inside, and suddenly she knows she wants nothing to do with it: it's no use trying to hold onto her life in this place.

48

*To upset everything every three or four years is
my notion of a happy life*

It is dark, Connie has to get out, has to flee the claustrophobic house. She enters the garden, its wild scary depths in the black, her long hair blowing about. The wind roars in the trees like the heft of a great soul passing; all is hostile, telling those caught within it to get away, get out. The glow of Mel's cottage is like a beacon in the black. Connie bangs loud on his door, calls his name. Pulls him from it, licks the tip of her tongue down his forearm.

'Out here?'

'Yes. Now.'

Why is it with Connie that only when she's doing something bad or irregular or wrong does that feeling of absolute power, and control, come shooting out with a whoop?

'You wild sweet thing, you!'

Out, out, running across open land, hand in hand, houses saucering the wide space. Giggly, making it to the sandpit. Needing risk, needing ridiculousness, Connie cannot explain it, she just needs to crack open her life, upset the apple-cart – she's never upset anything in her life! In the roguish wind she's pulling Mel towards the earth, scattering her Roger Viviers, her Marni cardigan, peeling everything off.

It doesn't work. Mel grates, he cannot come, it's all

wrong; Connie's thinking of Cliff, her future with him, her new hate; Mel is withdrawing, his spirit leaving her, he can feel the vast sigh of it.

'Well, that was no good,' he says. 'No good at all. You weren't there and neither was I.' He falls back. 'At least, I suppose, you aren't like my good lady wife. Dead inside. And if you forced her into it she'd just grind her teeth and send out waves of revulsion, hate.'

'How vile. You poor thing.'

'I need a woman who wants me, wants *it*.'

Connie giggles a kiss, draws Mel to her, slings her legs about him trapping him tight. 'There are lots of women like her. But not me, mister, not me!' She thinks of her friends, more than a few, who've never been warmed through by a man; would prefer not to do it at all but must, of course must; she thinks of all the vast dishonesty and pretence. And for years that was her.

'Thank God you're not like that shrew of a thing, thank God. I thought they all were. I need you, Connie.'

'Oh, you poor, scarred thing, you.' She kisses him between the eyes in a vast soothing. Pulls back. 'But do you honestly think a man and a woman should be together? Really? Truly?'

'For me, it feels like it's the core to my life.' Very quiet, very serious. 'You reminded me of that. You woke me up.'

Connie props up on her elbow and sighs. 'Oh, we're just a couple of battered old warriors, aren't we? You with your teeth-grinding wife, me with Cliff.'

Mel puts his arms behind his head. 'He's got no balls, that one.'

'What do you mean?'

'Well, when a man's got none of the earth in him, the wild streak, you say he's got no balls. When he's sort of tamed, removed, civilized beyond belief. And nasty with it. It's not a pleasant combination, and a lot of men have it.'

'And you're *not* tamed, mister?'

'No. Not quite! He's cold-hearted, Con.' Mel shivers. 'As for me, I'm all for a warm heart, for being warm-hearted in love, living with a warm heart, fucking with it. Loving your cunt, cunt, lovely cunt with it! Cherishing the whole damned lot of it.' He holds her close, places his hand between her legs in a kind of benediction, strokes, enters with a soft finger, her stomach dips. 'Can you feel it? Can you? The warmth?'

'Yes, yes, and I love you for that! Every single bit of you,' and Connie nestles up to him, feeling small and enfolded as they lie there under a vast bedspread of rare London stars. Mel kisses her. He's never been completely keen on mouth kisses, it's a peculiarity of his past, but not Connie's, oh no. She's taught him that the kiss can be the most intimate, transgressive act of the lot, if done right; that you can brush each other's souls in the touch.

'Let's be together.' He pulls away suddenly, speaking with the solemnity of ceremony. 'What do you say? You and me. Let's try it. Are we mad? We're mad.'

'Really?' Connie's eyes prick with tears. 'You can't mean it?'

'I'll get a divorce. Get clear. I hate all these things, courts, judges . . . but I'll do it. For you. To lure you out.'

'Of what?'

'All this.' He looks about him, shakes his head.

Connie's eyes fill, giddy with release and relief; with a firm footing from this point. She starts babbling, scarcely believing, she will have no money, Cliff won't give her any and, besides, she wouldn't take it, she's not that type, she has a little in the bank, yes, a year's worth perhaps, and some jewellery, she could sell it, she'll do that, doesn't know how much she'll get but she'll make it work, all of it, yes yes! Then she stops abrupt: 'You're laughing at me.'

Mel looks at her, straight into her. 'I don't laugh at you. Ever. It's the one thing I do not do.'

'I often think you laugh at me, like you can't quite believe it. Believe *me*.'

'Oh, I used to think you were just a bit of old wonderclout, before I knew you. I used to see you in the garden. You were noted, believe me, madam, from the moment I began this job. The crippled banker's wife, too young for all this. With the sad eyes that wanted something else but the husband never noticed, of course.'

'Uh-uh. Spool back. A bit of wonder-what?'

'Wonderclout. It means something showy but worthless. But no, oh no, you are quite something else. I know that now.' He holds his hand in reverence over Connie's heart. 'You have courage, and wildness, and goodness, and I never would have guessed. But I can see it now, all of it. I honestly didn't think anyone like you was left. I was so . . . flinched.'

Connie's heart is flung wide, wide open into the restless dark.

49

Arrange whatever pieces come your way

The clarion call of summer, Connie can feel it in the lovely lightness of the air. Cliff has decided upon their annual holiday. The *Ionika*, his newly finished beast of a super-yacht, for six weeks. They will sail the Caribbean. His family will join them from Connecticut. Connie feels the familiar choke of entrapment as he talks; always one's life arranged for one, always the wheels set in motion by someone else and it feels like it was ever thus.

But last night . . .

In the cold light of day she can scarcely believe what transpired. Did Mel really mean it? Can it actually work? Is she fooling herself? She'll sell some jewellery and that will make it fine, all fine, of course. Hello? What planet is she on?

Cliff is talking about how many cooks they'll need to hire for the yacht. Two? Three? They're driving through the suburbs to get to the outer reaches of London, a client's lunch. They are driving through a place she's never been before. What is next in her life? Connie so often feels there is no next, it's been such a familiar subtext to her adulthood. She stares out the window in the stalling traffic. It is as if dismalness, greyness, scruffiness, defeat have soaked through everything. The shops, the pavements, the pebbledash houses, net curtains, the clusters of satellite dishes: not a scrap of beauty in sight. A life with utterly no beauty in it . . . she couldn't imagine it. Living among it. How pressed down they must all feel, here, in a place like this. What on earth do they think of something like Kensington Palace Gardens, Cheyne Walk, the grand sweep of Lansdowne Crescent? The cherry blossoms in spring, shedding their petals like paper snow and how she loves to twirl in it; the twinkly Christmas trees lining the lampposts of Portobello on crisp December nights. Would they ever venture into her world? From that, to this.

Could she? Could she possibly? For surely Mel would have to leave his job; Cliff and his garden cronies wouldn't countenance his staying, they'd drum him out. Out of the garden, out of the area, out of their sight. So. They'd be forced to live somewhere far more affordable, like here, perhaps. Right. And their child, if they had one, would go to its local primary then its local comp, a grammar if they're good enough but are there any in these parts? No, they're all beyond London's inner reach, she's heard that; so, impossible, unless they move out and could they afford all the tutoring on top of everything else? Connie looks around her, trying to imagine the brave new options right at the start of their child's school life: perhaps one of those failing primaries with a plethora of free school meals and English as a second language for most. She experiences a flash of it: the narrowing of choice, the despair of it. The corrosiveness of envy suddenly seeps into her soul; she gets it.

The sleek panther of a car stops at traffic lights. A

posse of black kids in hoodies slap its windows as they cycle past. Connie yelps, Cliff tells the driver to run the red. 'Fast,' he snaps. 'Cunts.' So much anger, unspoken, struggling for articulation in this place; so much anger from the lot of them; everyone elbowing each other, jostling and lashing out, all the sharpness and unease and fret. Oh no, she couldn't live here, in a place like this, the future of England, surely not. But perhaps she must. Connie suddenly feels like a mouse in God's almighty paws – free me or eat me – she doesn't know what.

She just wants to be back in her dear Notting Hill, now, her lovely dipping place with its bespoke little gems of shops, her gym tucked into its darling cobbled street, her flower supplier in the cannily transformed toilet block, everything she could ever want. Lidgate's with the best meat in the land, Clarke's deli, the Electric, the glorious Gate cinema, the raffish delights of her Friday rummages on the 'Bello, pedis at the Cowshed, hefty gift books from Daunt's, even her chai lattes from Starbucks and you'd never get a chain like that in these parts. A life without her chai lattes, how would she cope! The vast seductive thrill of her neighbour-hood . . . the expansive sense of chuff she has dwelling in it. Connie looks out at the sullen, suspicious faces clocking their car now, its muggable occupants, wondering where it's going, if it will stop, if they'd get a chance.

No, no, she couldn't. But Mel, a new life . . .

England my England! she thinks. But which *is* my England? Which do I want? Suddenly overloaded with uncertainty, and Connie knows that a not-knowing is the most debilitating of states. She flops back in her seat and shuts her eyes, feeling like her life all of a sudden is a leaky wooden ship finally giving way to the water . . . all her dreams rushing out.

50

Alone, I often fall down into nothingness. I must push my foot stealthily lest I should fall off the edge of the world into nothingness

Home, to a crisp e-mail from her sister, Emma, who is a good bit older than herself. She is to be whisked away to her family's cottage in Scotland, for two weeks, her father will not take no for an answer and frankly, little sis, neither will the rest of us. Connie feels as she always does around this time of the year, constantly shuffled on the chessboard, a pawn to everyone else. She has to choose . . . has to face Cliff . . . cannot. It's like none of them quite trusts her by herself: where she would go, what she would do, in what way she'd uncurl, be lost to the lot of them.

She forwards Cliff her sister's e-mail, cc'ing Emma and all her family on it. It's for all of them to decide but she knows what will come to pass. Cliff is trapped. He cannot go against her family. He has always been slightly intimidated by them, their fluidity in the upper echelons of the English world. Their ease with wellies and smelly dogs and pheasant shoots, wretched yomping in forests after Sunday roasts; all that jolly grubbiness in country houses, dog hair on couches, ponies and hunting, collected Shakespeares in kitchens, too much drink. The English do wealth differently and he will never be a part of it. He's always sensed they tolerate him but don't particularly like him; he could never go down to the pub with his father-in-law and have a rousing chat over a pint. Connie's father is a fulsome man of great and spilling appetites, Cliff is not. All Protestant discipline and control to the father's blowsy Catholicism and sentiment.

'Whatever. You will fly out to meet with my own family, as soon as Scotland is done.' Cliff's brisk reply to the lot of them.

He is staying later and later at work, burying himself in it. The money is rolling in like never before, audaciously, in this financial climate. The PR consultant has been called in again to expand the charitable portfolio; to shore up the image, get him in the *FT* mag's 'Diary of a Somebody' and be smart about it. Cliff has said to Connie in the past that the best of his breed succeed with utter madness, and a touch of coldness, and a singular disdain for their clients – all of which must be masked, superbly. He does, he is supremely good at it, and as he feels his wife slipping from him he is even more ruthless with it all and ever more successful. For he has to succeed in at least one aspect of his life.

At night he plays poker with Marichka until 1 a.m. with a strange camaraderie between them both, long after Connie has retired. She can picture them like this in thirty years' time, still playing their cards, up all night. They're like an old married couple who've not had sex for decades and rarely talk about much, but vibrate so intimately upon one another that it's moving, settled, right; they know by instinct each other's thoughts, wants. Cliff raised Marichka's salary so she can gamble on it – she was losing so much to him, every night, and he was demanding she pay up. Connie was furious. Her husband was getting deader, colder, more competitive, with everything; removing himself completely from anything to do with a warm heart. Connie could no longer bear it. When she is back from her holiday she will leave him. She must, yes, she tells herself. His family will be around him. That will be a buttress to his anger. Yes, it will work.

Perhaps.

She glances at her latest black box from Net-A-Porter, still unopened on her bed. She slips off its satiny ribbon.

51

Outside the trees dragged their leaves like nets through the depths of the air; the sound of water was in the room and through the waves came the voices of birds singing

A soft pitter-pat of rain like a blanket over them both. Mel is asleep in his bed, in Connie's arms, the cup of her foot on his calf. It is that sleep of a man found. Her arms wing him tight and she breathes in his dreaming, of what? He wakes with a start.

'What if I had a child?' she asks.

He sighs. 'It seems a wrong and bitter thing to bring a child into this crazy world right now. Would you really want to? Can't you feel it? All the agitation, un-happiness, fret.'

'Oh, don't say that, don't!' A glittery quiet. 'I might be going to have one.' No one talks, as if the very air is digesting the news. Connie looks Mel deep in the eyes, all her dreams poised on the wings of those words.

'No.'

'Maybe, I don't know. It's too early. But I might.' Connie places his hand on her belly, smooths his fingers out. 'Are you pleased?'

'I'm pleased that you're pleased.'

'Then you don't really want me! You don't really want this.'

'No, no, Connie, I didn't say that,' Mel protests. 'I'm just not sure I want it growing up among . . . this. This world. Envious and raging. Feeling like life is constantly unfair, through no fault of its own. Never able to compete because its prospects haven't been decided at three, four – at that blinking nursery down the road, because we could never afford it. Everything is still so weighted by class, *still*, oh yes. All this, all around us! Look at our government, look where they all came from. It's so difficult to reinvent yourself in England, even now. More so, perhaps. Yes, Connie, I really do believe that. I could never crack the code – and I wouldn't want to. But our child might. It's bloody hard. And then who'd want to be these people, really? Who? Are they happy? I don't think so. I've seen too much. Heard it, as I'm wheeling my barrow past.'

'We don't have to stay here!' Connie grabs Mel's shoulders. 'We could go to South Africa. Australia. Somewhere fresh. Younger. Wilder. Closer to the sky and the earth. Where no one knows us. We could become something else!'

'We could,' Mel says slowly.

'I was born in Australia, you know. When Dad was a diplomat. I've never really thought about it because we moved on when I was two. I haven't a single memory of it, have never been back. But I'm sure I could get a visa. Perhaps.'

'I don't care what I do. I just know I can't stay here, after everyone knows. *If* everyone knows. All the men. And they will, eventually. I'm just waiting for it all to explode.'

'Tell me you want a child, Mel, tell me you have optimism, and hope. Still. Please.'

Connie is begging him, Mel is shaking his head, trying to get his head around it, the whole lot of it. 'If we could not live for money,' he says, quiet. 'If we could just live for something else . . . anything but that. Is it possible, Con? I don't know, in this world. All these people around us, so depleted in their souls, so greedy and grasping and unsettled by it. Too busy ever to live for anyone else. Even to notice. What do they live for, what? Really? Besides a vast accumulation of personal wealth?'

Thunder rolls across the sky like a series of bombs being dropped. Flint is in the air. Connie sits up like a dog, alert. They both listen to the rain getting heavier, dispersing the scent of the earth, pummelling the slate of Mel's roof.

Connie flings back her head and breathes it in deep.

'You really are a child of the earth, aren't you?' Mel chuckles, pulling her back. 'I bet Cliff never, ever noticed that. How much you need it.'

52

I am in the mood to dissolve in the sky

The rain is heavy now, the sky dark; Connie can smell it all, flinting her alive. She has a sudden desire to rush out into it. She looks at Mel and tilts her head enquiringly, giddy with the prospect of it, the challenge. Mel holds his breath, laughs in disbelief. His girl has slipped outside with a wild heavy laugh, utterly naked, out onto the central lawn of the garden in the pummelling wet, holding up her breasts to the drenching sky and spreading her arms and twirling about. 'Come on! No one's about. It's ours, ours, we own it for tonight!'

Mel laughs, what the heck, and dashes out, naked and white. He grabs Connie's slithery hands, runs her to a tree, rams her up against it in the gushing wet then tips her into wet leaves, wet earth, and takes her like an animal, quick, short, sharp, her slippery legs locked tight around his back.

Later, after a bath, Mel holds a towel over the springy hair of Connie's cunt and just keeps it there, still, in gratitude. She farts. Whoops with embarrassment.

'Hey, don't be silly. You shit and you piss, here, and here, just like an animal. Just like me, just like all of us. That's life. But what I can't abide – what I absolutely cannot abide – is what that bastard did to you once.' His fingers curl over Connie healing scars. 'How dare he violate you like that,' he says, turning her over and stroking the flesh of her rounded cheeks, the languid dip into her thighs. 'You've got the most beautiful arse that ever existed. Ever. Full stop. He had no right. It's criminal. Abuse.' Connie laughs, Mel is deadly serious. 'You should have flowers down here, daisies and snow-drops, not padlocks.'

Connie pushes him away, laughing, it's all gone, all in the past, she is entirely someone else; she looks at her watch, she will have to get back. Has to pack for Scotland. They're both suddenly quiet, as if each of them can feel the weight of separation; and both can sense it will be a reckoning of some sort.

'Do you mind me going away?'

'You have to do what you have to do,' Mel says, calm, quiet. 'It will make us or break us, I know that.'

'I thought it might be a good way to begin a severing . . . with Cliff. I do want a child. It might be a canny way of . . .'

'. . . letting everyone slip into believing a few lies, perhaps?'

'Yes.'

'And could you raise a child under his roof?'

'If you didn't take me away, then yes. I'd have to. He'd raise it as his, I guess. I don't think he'd be averse to it, actually, as long as he didn't know whose it was. There's a lot to think about.'

'And where would I take you? If I did take you . . .'

'Anywhere! Just away from here.' Connie's heart is fluttering in panic. What is she doing, what train is she setting in motion, what does she actually want here and she doesn't completely know; the panic of indecision, the vocation of procrastination, uncertainty, that has plagued her whole life. Goodness, obedience, weighing on her like a vice.

'I'm not making things difficult for you, Con, I just want to find out what you're after – but I don't think you really know yourself.'

No, no, she doesn't! Her eyes at him now tell Mel that.

'I'm not keen on being a kept man, either. By you, by anyone. My pride wouldn't allow it.'

'I know that!'

'I'd have to work. But it wouldn't be the life you're used to.'

'I love you for that. That you'd want to work . . . for us.' So much in her head, so much to work out, all, all when she's back. 'I just want to sleep with you, Mel, for one full night. Can I? Before I go. Just . . . sleep and then wake up with you next to me. I need it.'

'But how?'

'I'll work it out.'

And with that Connie is gone, swallowed by the scrubbed air, the wet black, her pale skin swiftly vanished in the dark.

53

And it was awfully strange, he thought, how she still had the power, as she came tinkling, rustling, still had the power as she came across the room

Connie bursts through the back door in a flurry, hair still wet, clothes crumpled, cheeks flushed. Cliff is reading a new history of Lincoln, champagne glass in hand. He's appalled, horrified at the vast unhinged sight of his new wife.

'Look at your hair – your clothes! Where have you been?'

'In the garden. It was so wild and wonderful with all the thunder and the lightning. The sky came roaring down. Did you hear it, Cliffy, did you? I was stuck and then just thought sod it! I ran out into the rain with no clothes on! Can you believe it? Couldn't resist.'

Cliff cannot comprehend. Any of it. His wife of the past few weeks, her new body, tallness, wildness, laugh, this crazed reckless confidence. 'You are mad. You must be. You are going mad. Suppose anyone saw. The gardener!'

'Well, he would have got the absolute fright of his life and run off as fast as he could. Quite completely spooked and utterly not able to cope. No one is as mad as me,' she declares, laughing and taking the champagne glass from Cliff's hand and tipping it up in an extravagant sip.

Cliff stares at the long, exposed throat of his wife, transfixed. Appalled. Admiring. She looks so glowing and healthy, so brimming with life. Unbound. After the stasis of this house, their new life. Perhaps this is what works, perhaps there will be a lot more of this. Perhaps he can use it.

'Do you like your body?' he asks, quite dispassionately.

'I *love* it,' she proclaims joyously, thinking of Mel's declaration that she has the best arse that ever existed. Cliff remembers back to a very different body, a very different wife.

'What's caused this sudden change in you? Running out into the rain, putting on weight, laughing like a mad woman or a naughty child. Is it the summer's heat? Anticipation of a holiday, desire for sensation, change, boredom, what?'

'All of it! The whole damned lot! Should I change for you, my darling, become very quiet, and meek, is that what you want? How you'd like it. The little kitten in her pretty collar, all obedient.'

'Oh, don't bother. You almost communicate a thrill to me.'

Connie is thrilled, yes, thrilled – to feel the bonds snap. She couldn't deny it. She refills Cliff's glass, hands it across, and gets one for herself.

'I want to get my video camera out. Like old times. Come on, Con, come on. Just this once. The Emin neon . . . panning across to you . . .' – he mimes a camera close on her cunt – 'you're on my bed . . . waiting, wide, knowing not what . . . yes . . . your new magnificence.'

Cliff clutches his wife's thigh, her waist, and inhales deep. As if he is breathing in life itself.

54

Now begins to rise in me the familiar rhythm

Emma is driving across to London to pick up Connie. She loves a long drive. They will stay the night, leave at the crack of dawn, meander up the motorway, stop at friends near York. Excellent, all of it. For Connie has a plan.

'I'll put you up in a hotel, Emma, the Dorchester, Claridge's, whatever you want. You just have to give me one night to myself. Pick me up from home say, 3.30, drop me around the corner, have a quick cuppa and then head off to wherever, to wallow in your lovely luxury. Then come back for me the next morning. Nine a.m., on the dot.'

'Why? What's going on? Is there bonking involved? Have you got a fella? *Nee*sie.'

'Yes. Yes yes!'

Shocked silence, down the line, then, 'Well, I can't say you don't need it. Just be careful, all right.'

'Thank you, Em, thank you.'

They will get their sleep. Staying in the Portobello Hotel, Connie's always wanted to try it. It was always too small, crammed, fusty for Cliff; not grand enough. It's where Kate Moss and Johnny Depp had their champagne bath; she's always wondered what it is like. It will be perfect. Connie gets a shudder in her belly just thinking of it. They will come at separate times, yes, no one has to know. She wants Emma to meet Mel, too, it is all part of the plan. To sever ties with Cliff's life, to veer her man into her family's path.

He's reluctant.

'You have to. You must.' As petulant as a child. 'And I will have to dress you. Scrub you up.'

'*What?*'

'I'll take you to Paul Smith, get you a suit.' Connie purrs at the thought. 'It's just down the road. Twenty minutes of your time!'

Mel backs back.

'You come in by yourself. Just be there, mister. One p.m. On the dot. Choose, then I'll slip in at the end and pay for it. I'll be there looking for socks for Cliff, no one will know. It's ingenious. Yes, yes! Because after Emma you'll have to meet my parents, my father, and you can't be looking like this. Maybe for her, but not for them. God, no. They wouldn't cope.'

Connie's like a force of nature now, standing there, blazing with it. She has purpose, suddenly, layers are peeling from her, layers and layers from a long-silted life. Remembering a dynamism, an energy, a fierce will from young womanhood she thought long lost. Scurried over by life, but now it's back.

Mel cannot resist.

55

To love makes one solitary, she thought

Two sisters, side by side on the sunken, red velvet couch of the Portobello Hotel's sitting room overlooking its garden. Silverware in readiness on the coffee table, fine bone china in front of them. French doors open, revealing a cram of luxuriant green beyond a pale gravelled path.

The sisters wait in brittleness. They are the only ones in the room at four o'clock. Connie will not reveal much of her Mel to Emma despite persistent questioning. She wants her sister to meet him clean of all perception. Emma, a successful GP, has always conveyed the impression she's slightly irritated by her younger, prettier, more vivid sibling, all Connie's life she has felt this. She has told Emma Mel's name and that he's a gardener but not much else.

'So, you'd really like to be plain old Mrs Mel Jones instead of Mrs Clifford Carven the Third, would you?'

'Yes.'

'Think carefully about this, Neesie. Very carefully. No more fresh flowers and eyebrow threadings. No more weekly manis, reflexology, waxing. Opera opening nights, gone, Babington weekends, suppers at the Wolseley. All vanished. No more holidays in the Seychelles and the south of France, private planes and super-yachts. You'll have to dye your hair at home, by yourself. No, hang on, you won't have time because you'll be working so blooming hard; you'll have grey soon enough on your temples just like me – look. And you'll have to learn to cook. No, sis, an oven is not for storage and gourmet does not mean scrambled eggs. You'll have to scrub the toilets. Take out the rubbish. You'll be worn down, that's what life with him will do to you. Wear you completely down until you're all lined and saggy from it. It'll all be on your face. And then, of course, you'll come running to Daddy, darling Daddy, for help.'

'I will not. You have no idea, Em, of any of this.'

'Why on earth do you want to do it? Keep this Mel person as your fuck buddy, by all means, Cliff would probably be happy with that. But don't take it any further, for all our sakes, please, don't.'

'But I feel alive, Em, like I'm in the middle of something so exciting and fresh and energizing and glorious – creation, a new world – like everything is so wondrous and clean. Yes, clean. Spare, ready. For the first time in my adult life.'

'Oh, stop your babbling. You're in love. It will pass. Then reality will sink in and you'll both be stuffed. You'll get over him quickly enough. You both will.'

At that point Mel walks in. Transformed in his new attire. Lean, innately graceful, as if he has been wearing these kinds of clothes all his life. Connie realizes with a little smile that he could go anywhere, like this, that women would always look. He's inherently arresting and doesn't know it. A bonus. And far more naturally elegant than Cliff ever was.

But he's nervous. Brusque with her sister, in his greetings and small talk, not allowing any of his beguiling looseness, softness. Inherently wary of what she will make of him, his motivations, his greed for whatever she's got. He speaks rougher in Emma's presence, more street, almost as a challenge to her to see how she'll take it.

He pours the tea then sits back and watches the two women. So physically alike yet so different. The older one like a hessian sack with bits of straw hanging out; she's been unhappily married for several decades, Mel knows that and can see it in her face; it's all settling into sourness, especially the downward curve of her lips. He cannot imagine his sunny Connie ever, ever becoming that. No wonder she's irritated by her sister; Connie has a lightness she never has, it's obvious. He watches the two of them with the power of silence and containment and distance, as he always does in company, that Connie felt so attracted to from the first sight. To be so unneedy of anyone else; Emma senses it too.

'Is this all worth the risk?' she suddenly asks, abrupt. The headmistress who's had enough.

'What risk?' Mel responds calmly, nonchalantly. Ready for the gladiatorial combat and knowing where he's placed.

'My sister stands to lose a lot here.'

'Perhaps she stands to gain a lot, too. She comes to me for a bit of warmth and I give it to her.' A dirty smile, a shrug. 'I think she needs it. So what's it to you? She's a grown woman, what say do you have in her life? She's strong. Tough. She can make up her own mind.'

Emma sighs, infuriated, and turns to her sister. 'You can't go making a mess for us all to clean up, Connie.'

'Haven't you perhaps made a bit of a mess of your

own life?' Mel challenges. 'I hear you're staying together for the sake of the kids, that it's a poisoned house. So why deny your sister the right to happiness and freedom here? If you can't have it yourself. Is that fair? What's the subtext of this?'

'It is fair, because the so-called "happiness and freedom"' – Emma puts up her fingers, signalling inverted commas – 'you talk about so lovingly is with you. And what can you offer her, I wonder? Really? After all that she's got. She's had. Almost her entire adult life.'

'What can I offer her?' Mel's got his cheeky face on, Connie can guess something of what's coming next and Emma will not like it. 'Great sex' – Mel grins at the thought – 'yep. But hey, don't ask me. Ask her yourself what I can offer her. Look at her. She's changed. Her whole body, her face, her entire demeanour. It's all there.' Mel is throwing down the gauntlet to Emma with a kind of grimy sensuality Connie's never seen before; it's thrilling and mortifying all at once. She throws up her arms as if she gives up entirely at this point. Mel winks at her; the two naughty schoolkids at the back of the class.

Emma stands brusquely. 'I can find my own way out.' Turns to them both, livid.

'All I want to say is, I doubt whether either of you will find that it's been worth it in the long run. In the cold hard light of day, when everything else is gone from your lives. You, Mr Jones, your job – in a climate where it's extremely difficult to find work. And you, Connie, well, everything. Every single thing that you've got. Husband, house, clothes, respectability, friends, social life, shops. You have a very comfortable life. Very,

very comfortable. Everyone thinks so. And you've grown extremely used to it. Plus your husband is a cripple who needs you. Have you thought of how this looks? You just need to wake up.'

Emma brisks out.

'Nine a.m., on the dot. We have a long drive ahead of us.'

Without looking back.

56

But when the self speaks to the self, who is speaking? The entombed soul, the spirit driven in, in, in to the central catacomb; the self that took the veil and left the world – a coward perhaps, yet somehow beautiful, as it flits with its lantern restlessly up and down the dark corridors

A tiny room, all bed. A night of rough sex; sharper, more urgent, more terrible than ever before. Walloping, grubby, exhilarating, oh yes; Mel is demanding with her, reckless, more than he's ever been but it's all the more exciting because of it; Connie is passive, consenting, his supine slave. He's flipping her over, licking her arse, her cunt, coming into them both; she's grabbing his penis and sucking him off, voluptuously, deep, and she usually hates that. It's as if they're both trying to brand each other with the memory of their touch; to wipe the vast soiling of the afternoon off, to prove to Emma that yes, this is what binds them, yes, this is what they've got – gloriously – and so what? Connie learns so much about herself that night, opening herself wide, wider, begging for it, everywhere, in every orifice, coming to the very heart of the beast of herself.

And for the first time in her life it is the man with her, in her, in front of her, behind her during sex who is at the forefront of her mind. She's not thinking of anyone else, she's not lost in a different scenario entirely. She's utterly present with him, bared, her base, sensual self, flaring herself wide, supremely naked and unashamed, with no toys or games or props. What a triumph this feels like. To be so present. An arrival into a new life. The one ridiculous taboo left, Connie thinks: sex as an utterly natural, animal, vital, spiritual, instinctive act. Sex of the earth. So removed from what it has become everywhere else; in every other instance of her adult life.

Deep in the night, the first night they've ever shared, Connie wakes to the wing of Mel's arm cupping her sleep, his torso curled around her and his hand balled in the softness of her groin. The sanctity of it, the sanctity of shared sleep, and a vast smile filling her up.

Morning, she is awoken by lips on her eyelids. A silk slip is almost ripped in two, panties are lost; no matter. The day's finding its feet; behind a first scrim of cloud there's a higher heaven and she smiles at the optimism in the sky. Time is marching on swift, too swift, towards nine o'clock; when they both must find the world, burrow out . . .

'You will keep the tenderness for me, won't you?' she whispers, forehead to forehead, as a tear slips down her cheek.

'Yes.'

'It's what I love about you the most.'

'What?'

'That you're not afraid of tenderness. That it's deep in you, through you. You're not afraid of the feminine. It's what distinguishes you from all the other men. Any man I've ever had.'

She holds her breathing quietly to him, collecting his smell, and then he is vanished, just like that, back, back to his work.

And Connie must go on.

57

For pleasure has no relish unless we share it

Hills nudging the belly of the sky, mountains pushing up into cloud, slopes whooshing down into road. Connie is ensconced within the sturdy stone walls of the family's West Highland house that envelops with reassurance against the bash of the wind and the wet. The clouds move over a distant mountain like the drawing of a stately curtain and the weather is all symphonied as it thunders and spits and clears and repeats. Connie loves it here, gulps it up, always feels strong in it.

A symphony of people, too. Varied visitors from down south, a tumble of laughter and drinking and dogs and kids and talk and as Connie sits among it all she knows this time here will set her on a path. One way or another. Emma does too. They're wary around each other, not wanting to pick at the scab of the man who insulted the elder sibling so fruitily and Connie doesn't have an answer for it except that Emma insulted him just as much. So Connie sits back as Mel does, and watches all the males around her, all the family friends, and imagines sleeping with every one of them. Gauges their tenderness, wonders if she'd be surprised by any of them; none would rival Mel she knows that and she misses him, searingly, so much. Wishes he was there, amid this happy raucousness, this roguish air and yelling light.

Yet Connie doesn't want to go back to London now she is here, under this piebald sky in this humble, salt-scoured place. Its people seem so unhinged, jittery, suspicious, brusque; there's no kernel of stillness, no quiet to any of them. Except Mel. The city presses down on her, she knows that when she's apart from it; the sheer hardness of living in it, of just getting by in its great press of people. What must it be like to have no money in it, she can't imagine. The corrosiveness of envy, yes, that's Mel's expression and she gets it now, as she worries at the knot of ahead, how it could possibly work.

Connie walks the audacious, ancient landscape around her, often, rain spitting at the loch, and every time she looks the water's colour has changed in the shifting, wind-blown light. But here, here, she is alive. Flushed. Clear. Here, deep in her bones, she knows what she wants. One simple thing.

Happiness.

Has a blind craving for it now, needs to be assured of it. Connie knows through experience that this means not letting anyone else shape her life. She creates it, she alone, she must. This is what it means to be a woman today. A vivid, dynamic, present, modern, truly happy woman.

It's taken her a long time to realize that.

58

*I feel so intensely the delights of shutting oneself
up in a little world of one's own, with pictures
and music and everything beautiful*

Two blue lines on the white stick and of course, of course, Connie knew it. In the toilet of the cottage, among paperbacks and rosettes and prints of grouse, she holds her palm in wonder to the little thrummer inside her brewing in its sac. Collector of her food, her air, her energy, her happiness, and she glows with it.

Her father summons her for a walk, it's their daily ritual. 'Coming, Papa!' As she calls him sometimes, which he loves.

It's cold, the backs of Connie's ears trap the chill and thud with hurt even in this, high summer. The wind fans the close loch and she balances her feet on a wide, wobbly stone as the breeze whips her and butts her and tries to push her off. She giggles with delight, won't be budged, and her father chuckles. How like a child she still is, always, with her ready laughter. She'll always have that in her and thank God for that, the high joy of it.

'A little dull for you, eh, going back to your big gloomy house after all this?' he remarks cheekily.

'Actually' – a pause – 'I'm not sure I want to go back, Daddy.'

'Oh. Is there something you want to tell me?'

'I'm going to have a baby.'

Connie's face shines with the telling, it's the first time

she's told this to anyone. It feels good, galvanizing, strong; so good she has to repeat it in astonishment. 'A baby!'

'Whose?'

'You don't know him.' Her smile is vast.

'Well then, that will work out nicely. You can present Cliff with an heir, liven up the house. No one will ask any pesky questions, I presume – things being so delicate in that department. Good all around, I guess?'

'I don't think I want to do that.' Connie frowns, stepping carefully off her rock.

'What?' Her father sighs. 'Fallen for this other bloke, have we?'

'I'm afraid so. Rather ridiculously, in fact.'

'Well, you'll get very little out of making a break. Cliff won't let you, you know that. You'll be quite savagely cut off.'

They're silent.

Her father puts his arm around his daughter, as he always does after a contretemps. 'I just hope for your sake you had a real man at last.'

Connie winces a laugh; she'd told her father while tipsy, early on in the relationship, that Cliff wasn't great in the sack and what do you know, he's remembered it. He's a sensual man and has always been open about the vivifying capacity of sex; wants it for his children as much as himself.

'I did, Daddy, I did, yes. And that's the trouble. I've never had one like him before. There aren't many of them about.'

'Good. Excellent. And he was a lucky man, my girl. He won't make any trouble for you, will he?'

'No, oh no. He . . . frees me. He lets me do what I want. I've never felt more capable . . . empowered . . . in my life!' The smile skips back.

'Do you want to be with this man, Neesie?'

A pause. Thinking of Cliff's fury, Emma's scorn.

'Yes.'

Firmer.

'Yes.'

Rain spits at the loch, Connie raises her face to a wild sky. She must get back, yes, resume her life, inform Mel of so much. She must hurry. The train, not the car this time. Trouble's brewing, there's news of riots, in the grim parts; a man shot dead by police in Tottenham; thank goodness she's not part of it. But she must rush back. Expectation blazing under her skin. Firm with it now. To begin a fresh way, at last.

As she waits, poised, in the wings of her life. To burst forth.

59

Life is not a series of gig lamps symmetrically arranged; life is a luminous halo, a semitransparent envelope surrounding us from the beginning of consciousness to the end

Catching sight of Mel from a distance at King's Cross Station and getting a tremor in her bowels deep inside her, like the beginning signal of an orgasm, because she's aching with want at the sight of him. Connie walks straight up to him and drinks him long on his lips.

'I'm taking you with me,' she says.

He drops his head, forehead to forehead, quiet.

'If it's what you want, ma'am. I've got nothing, you know that. Know what it means. I'll have to work, wherever we are. For you. For us. But it'll be a very different life.'

'I'm ready. I'll work, too. I want to. I don't know quite what yet, but I will. I need it. And hey, mister, you've got more than most men. You've got tenderness. That's all I need now. For the rest of my life.'

Connie looks at Mel, holds his hand to her belly, enfolds it with both of hers, three palms firm.

'There's a baby in here.'

Mel laughs, shakes his head. Looks at her: 'No'; she nods yes. Singing with it, singing inside; he bends and kisses the womb, with reverence.

'Where shall we go, little one?' he whispers. 'Where on earth?'

Connie shrugs, Mel laughs. Somewhere wild, fresh, that's all she knows. A new start. Far, far away from all this. From the people who are like frail little boats tossing unanchored in their restless seas, all of them. To give this little one a fresh start. Spring cleaning her own life, Mel's life, leaving everything behind, she doesn't need much, just a backpack and a few books. Walk-in wardrobes for every season? Excuse me? There'll be no need of six-inch heels and Tibetan lamb gilets any more, in a new existence, wherever it may be. Connie has begun with boldness: informed Cliff that no, she won't be making it to America and the yacht, that he must enjoy this time with his family by himself. She needs the break. They both do. Free! Free! No longer having to withstand the onslaught of his mother and his sisters who can never quite relinquish the notion that she's in it for the money, even now, post accident; Connie can always sense it. Free of the lot of it.

But how terrifying it seems: to contemplate an evacuation from one's entire life, its routines and exhaustions and cemented paths. How terrifying and simple and exhilarating all at once.

60

Oh, is this your buried treasure? The light in the heart

Emma has told her father about Mel, predictably, as soon as Connie left. He is coming down to London at once; through a rioting country, yes, pronto, because this needs sorting out. He had assumed his Neesie was talking about a man of means, but he is just a simple gardener. He has to meet the chap, talk with both of them. How could this man take care of his princess? His daughter's life so reduced and a baby coming, no, no, this will not do at all; he needs to fix it, fast.

Connie makes the booking. The Ledbury. A short walk. Two Michelin stars, rosy parquet, tall windows, thick curtains, smooth quiet. Neither man is keen, Mel less so.

Both greet each other warily and dive into stiff drinks. Small talk about life and work as the tasting menu is brought out, neither man knowing what such a thing is and Connie serving to them both, explaining, then sitting back with the withdrawn, sated stillness of the pregnant. But . . . an unfurling, from both of them. The wonder of that. Despite everything, she is witnessing the two most important men in her life bonding over their shared discombobulation, and laughing inwardly at it – what's a boudin, what's a velouté, teal, can't these things be in English for once? I say, give me a nice little Sunday roast any day. Pie and chips, thanks. Pickled eggs! Oooh, ploughman's lunch! Steak and ale! Mash! What does this all mean, Connie, come on, help us out. Ceviche. Kohlrabi. Kaffir lime. Explain, Neesie, drag us into this brave new world. Neesie, why do you call her that? Her nickname from when she was a baby, God knows why, Conneeee, Neesie, something like that. Waiter! And more drinks are ordered for them both.

'So. My daughter.' The elder man is suddenly cutting to the chase over his boudin of teal and grey partridge.

'Your daughter. Yes, sir. A fine lass.'

'And she's pregnant with your child.'

'Indeed. I have that honour, I do, yes.'

Connie can sense it: her father softening, despite himself, to the natural grace of this man, so smart in his suit, and decent, unshowy, with it; his simple good-ness leaking from him and her father's radar, honed over a lifetime of diplomacy, picking it up.

'Honour!' Her father looks at Mel, considering where to take this. Another sip. He's drinking a lot. Breaths held. Finally, a chuckle. 'So, how was it? She's a fine lass. Good, my boy? Eh?'

'Oh, yes. The best.'

'And with a woman who loves it, too – what a joy, what a treat. I can see it in Connie's flush, she's all shined up, isn't she, with happiness. The sheer joy of it.' He caresses her cheek. 'The happiest I've seen her in . . . what?' He's stuck, the drink's got to him at last and it takes a lot to get him to this point. 'Well done, lad, well done,' clapping Mel on the back. 'It's all a parent ever wants for their child . . . happiness. Now. To . . . to business.' Another sip. 'How old are you?'

'Thirty-six.'

'Well, you've got a good twenty, thirty years left in you then. Excellent, good, excellent. You've got skills, young man. You'll be fine, won't you, you'll get a job anywhere.'

'That I will. I've got the hard work in me if nothing else.'

'Good, good. And where will you two lovebirds be nesting?'

They look at each other, don't know.

Banging, suddenly, outside, then banging at the windows. The waiters yelling at the diners to get away from the glass, what, what's going on? Screams and shouts, they have to move to the restaurant's inner wall but it's too late – men and women in white are suddenly trying to barricade the front door with chairs. Mel stands, goes to help, what's going on? Connie's beating heart as she cups her belly, twisting tight.

Suddenly a loud smash, a tsunami of glass as the door is broken through and in scatter, what, fifteen, twenty men in hoodies and stockings, mostly black, wielding baseball bats, wine bottles, machetes, knives. 'Get down, get down!' they yell, throwing things about: plates, glasses, tables, trolleys, wanting to destroy the lot. Instinctively all the diners huddle to the floor. Mel rushes back to them both, the clientele now all under tables, racing hearts, scrambling to hide wallets, passports, watches and the rioters methodically working the room as if they've done this many times before, demanding jewellery, mobile phones, cash.

A young kid comes up to the three of them, about fourteen at the most, a smattering of down on his upper lip and he jerks up Connie's hand and rips off her vintage Rolex, grabs at her Wallis Simpson ring. 'Off, off!' he yells and Connie tries, can't. Mel attempts to intervene, a machete menaces, he flinches back. The rioter grabs Connie's hand and wrenches it, she screams with the vast pain, other kids behind him hold her men back with machetes, knives, and then the kitchen staff are flooding up with brooms, rolling pins, frying baskets but it's too late, there are not enough of them, they're overwhelmed. 'Where are the police?' 'Police!' People yell but they are gone, gone, to everywhere else where London's burning, but here? What? Who would have thought? In this beautiful, gracious room of two-hundred-a-head meals, the real world intruding, no, surely not. Impossible. But yes.

And then they've fled, just like that, the whole streamlined gaggle of them; off to Westbourne Grove, Portobello, who knows. Everyone emerges, shaking, taking out mobile phones and ringing loved ones and checking news and texting, trying to get cabs to get far far away from this place but no cabs will come. Their waiter with the lovely, wide Antipodean smile offers the three of them champagne and whisky to calm nerves, despite being robbed himself. 'I'll take the lot thanks,' says Connie's dad, grabbing two glasses and downing both.

'Onya, mate. You deserve it.'

Then the rumours circulate, the rioters are returning and all the diners are ushered downstairs now, to the toilets, quick. 'Lock yourselves in,' flurry the staff and obediently everyone splits along gender lines so Connie is separated. 'My father, my boyfriend,' she gasps. 'You'll be right, mate,' says the waiter with the wide smile as he ushers her further in.

Then a few minutes later the staff are back, ushering everyone out, to the wine cellar, a safer bet. Connie finds her men, presses close; 'She'll be right,' says a kitchen hand in his slow, calm, Australian drawl, 'I'm a boxing kangaroo, I'll look after you.'

And then they are safe, the police arrive, finally, and the good people of Notting Hill spill out, trembling, texting and calling afresh, crying, shaking their heads in disbelief, laughing with relief. Here? In dear old Ledbury Road, with Anya Hindmarch, Emma Hope and Brora within spitting distance? No, too close for comfort, far too close; the protective wall of affluence that has always protected them has been most savagely, impertinently breached. I say, the shock of it! Connie can't stop shaking, clutching her belly and rubbing it, begging her tiny, precious hoverer to be still, quiet, safe. Oh, what a traumatic jolt for such a little one, her blood is still racing, she wants out.

Mel puts his arm around her, sensing it. 'You OK?'

She nods, biting her lip. Mel puts his arm around her father, too. 'Now where were we before we were most rudely interrupted . . .' He shakes his head, looking around at all the milling people, the sirens, the police kitted out in their riot gear. 'Something about nesting, wasn't it?'

'As far away as possible, please.' Connie's voice wavers as she looks across at her kitchen hand, his easy smile, his sunny difference. He catches her eye and raises a hand in relief.

'Australia, perhaps. Yes.'

61

It is fatal to be a man or woman pure and simple: one must be a woman manly, or a man womanly

Clifford finally knows. Connie doesn't want to go near him, wants to stay exiled in Scotland, in Cornwall, but she must, he demands it; she is his wife. They are in the morning parlour with its emerald silk Earlham wallpaper by de Gournay which Connie swooned over when it was presented to her and now it leaves her dead, cold, as does this entire house. Her husband is like a hysterical child in it now, in this moment of realization, a mummy wrapped up in its bandages, come to life and flailing with it.

'I would have let you fuck a black man, a prostitute, a woman, anything, anyone; something that I could watch – or not' – he spits – 'if you'd *just asked*. Wasn't that enough? I was so good to you. Gave you everything. But . . . the gardener? *Him*. Out there. Under the nose of all my friends. All our world. Out there. Knowing. Laughing at me. Us.'

'No one knew.'

'They do now. Your little bit of fluff is walking around out there like a dog with a tin can attached to his tail. Hasn't anyone told you that?'

Connie shuts her eyes, no, no, Mel has not told her this. And he dreaded the eyes so much, that they would make it grubby, reduce it to its tawdry basics without knowing any of it.

Cliff bangs his fist on the wheelchair. Enraged he has not controlled this, enraged that his wife has so triumphantly slipped from his grasp. Enraged that it's that cunt of a gardener who took her from him, in his T-shirts and baggy shorts. Enraged that *she* took *him*. Wanted him. When he's got nothing in the world. Doesn't even own a car let alone a house. When she has all this.

'You'll get no money from me.'

Connie has gone over and over this moment in her head. She could get a lot, with a no-fault divorce, millions. Could get an exhilarating amount and be tied to Cliff, his vitriol and his hate, for the rest of her life. Her future bound to his for evermore. Everyone would know, and judge, and she would have to live with it. He would do his best to crush her – and Mel. To break her spirit utterly and spend whatever money it took to do it. She has seen it in other friends who dare to divorce their alpha male bankers; men determined to win no matter what. Her friend Perdita resorted to calling the police after domestic violence became commonplace; the female officer told her these high-end marital breakdowns in Kensington and Chelsea are the most brutal and savage of the lot – because the man is so supremely competitive and determined to destroy at any cost.

So. Connie could now fight for a huge payout from her crippled husband – or she could set herself free. To start afresh. Both of them. All of them.

She lifts her head high. 'Actually, Clifford, I don't want a penny from you. I've thought about this. It stains me. Your entire world does.'

He laughs in disbelief. 'You'll have to work. You have

no skills. What on earth could someone like you possibly do?'

Everything, of course, is disdain, belittling; everything she has ever tried in her life. It is time to leave, she has had enough. Connie raises an eyebrow, smiles, turns without a word.

Arrested by his snarl.

'I will humiliate you. I will tell the world what you have done, sexually. I will release the tapes on the Internet. Oh yes, I've got a lot. Even, you cunt, that night of the padlock. I'm not on it but you, oh you, most certainly are. Just watch me.'

Connie walks out, her hands clamped over her ears. Her racing heart, pounding, roaring in her chest.

62

*To tell the truth about oneself, to discover
oneself near at hand, is not easy*

How to cauterize him.

How to triumph magnificently from this bleakness. Is there any way? How to vanquish and rise up because she must. Or Connie will go mad, utterly mad from it. No money, no, not a cent, she will never ask; couldn't bear the court case and his brutal lawyers, the best of course, primed to crush her and nothing else; couldn't bear the years of emotional turmoil in his grip. You hate what you cannot be, and how Clifford hates Mel, with every fibre of his being, and her husband will drag his rival into this all too, consumingly, and their child in her belly. Connie couldn't bear the vast, extensive stain of it through her life. She's seen it in all those other banker divorces around her, so many now as the years roll on, the desire to eviscerate at any cost, to utterly destroy and humiliate.

Connie can't go down that path, can't.

So. She will leave with nothing. Free, at least. To work out how to triumph in all this, to wriggle her way free of Cliff's vast and swamping threat. To find a way to reclaim her narrative – *hers*, not his. Her equilibrium, her life.

63

*Odd affinities she had with people she had never
spoken to, some women in the street . . .*

Heathrow airport. Flight delayed, mechanical problems with Qantas. The plane is called 'Longreach'. Connie likes that, it's appropriate, they can do this. It's en route to Sydney; mechanics are on the tarmac, scurrying about.

In the departure lounge, weary resignation from the collected travellers chafing for a going home, a holiday, a new world or life. Mel is off wandering. Connie is sitting with a woman who has a boy, about twelve, who's buried in some game on his iPhone, and another woman with three boys scamping about and a baby. She hopes she's not sitting next to her on the flight. The baby, a girl, starts grizzling, the eldest son lifts the child from her pushchair and jiggles her in his arms, effort-lessly, with much chuff; a little man of the new world, Connie thinks, and how blooming to see it. She smiles at him.

'You're doing a good job there.'

The three women smile tentatively and flirt with small talk, filling up the waiting hours. The mother with the lone son lives in Paris – oh! – and is taking him to see the Barrier Reef; it's just the two of them in their life, they travel a lot; have just been to visit the boy's father, in London, have been to Uluru before this, years ago, and the Sydney Opera House. The woman with the cacophony of kids is heading out to visit her father for Christmas, she's Aussie but lives in Gloucestershire and her husband's following later, when his holidays begin. 'He's a GP, he never takes a break.' A grimace, but a smile with it.

'I'm going to live in Australia,' Connie announces quietly, rubbing her belly. 'We're starting afresh. A whole new adventure. Goodness knows if we'll like it.'

Exclamations, delight, from both the women.

'Oh, you'll love it! Especially the light,' says the one with the four kids.

'I think so, yes. I can't wait.'

The other woman pipes up. 'The thing about Australia is, and I've noticed this. No one can box you into a corner over there. Unless you want to be boxed in. And I just can't say the same about England, I honestly can't. It's why I don't live here any more.'

Connie looks at these two women, both older than her. They look so utterly normal, regular; thickening with age but comfortable with it, a bit scuffed of course but beautiful, strong, with their certainty and their strength. She wonders what their sexual lives have been, what regrets, bleaknesses, unlockings they have experienced; what humiliations and exhilaration and what vividness. Surely not, like her. Who knows? Who knows with anyone?

The secrets we all keep . . .

64

*I will not be 'famous', 'great'. I will go on
adventuring, changing, opening my mind and my
eyes, refusing to be stamped and stereotyped.
The thing is to free one's self: to let it find its
dimensions, not be impeded*

'I will humiliate you. I will release the tapes on the Internet . . .'

Hence this book. A woman bared. A normal, everyday woman who looks no different to any other, any woman, every woman, perhaps; she could be the woman in front of you in the supermarket line, at the bus stop, she could be any of us. So. All her darkness and light, all her deep raging secrets and ugliness and beauty and rawness and wants, glittery wants. That no one, perhaps, would ever know about.

Because Connie will no longer let a man dictate her story, nor quash it, nor control it nor represent it. This is who she is and she has found the courage, finally, to speak out. *This* is a woman's vulnerability. Her complexity. Her hiddenness and contradictions, her defiance and her daring. She knows there will be hatred and belittling and derision and scorn but still she writes on, and on. Because she is no longer afraid. Because she will not be objectified. Because she has to own her story, her truth – no one else.

65

The world is crammed with delightful things. I think young people make such a mistake about that – not letting themselves be happy. I sometimes think that happiness is the only thing that counts

A little fishing village on the cusp of the Pacific. Roaring light. All wondrous, strange, fresh. The trees shed their bark here but not their leaves; 'the ripping trees', Connie calls them, to Mel, in delight. So much delight! He has told her that at times he is afraid of all this, starting flush, the huge differences; but he believes in her being with him, in the peace of them being together and in the peace of their fucking and so they are here in this place. Where people smile when they talk. Where you cannot be boxed in. Where the top schools in this country, in terms of academic results, are all free, state. The optimism of a meritocracy! Where there's not the bitterness of envy like in England because anyone can be anything here, if you work hard enough; they both hear it all the time but, most importantly, they see it.

Connie rubs her growing belly, often. Looks across to the venerable mulberry tree in the unfenced park next door that's like a benevolent god with its long arms dipping down, dispersing its joy to all in the know. She watches the tree shivering, the local children high in its limbs, arms and legs and blue-swabbed faces briefly bursting out only to be drawn back inside the green depths to more juicy baubles of sweetness, and yet more, higher and higher as the lower branches are denuded and she smiles vast, listening to shrills and shrieks of triumph and it's pure exhilaration, to bottle, to pass on to the next generation, and the next. Her little one will be a part of all this. This freedom, this hurting light. And she is glad, so immensely glad of that.

For Connie, this is a place where the eye rests. Yes, the talking dark of night is crammed with feral screams and rustlings and hoots and squawks, possums and foxes and cockatoos, kookaburras and lorikeets, but by day she sits on her balcony, writing out her truth. Virginia, dear, wise Virginia, her guide and barometer of honesty in all this. The words prowl until they are written, for Connie will no longer let a man dictate the parameters of her life and with that resolve comes a vast relief. She is swept clear of Cliff. Of all that he threatens. She has found a voice. And so the happiness plumes through her in this tiny old teapot of a weather-board house that rings with its foreign air and light and squawks.

How strange and terrifying it must have been for those first British settlers, Connie thinks, as if an alien god had created this world to astound, to terrify: it sounds like it hurts to be in this place. She comes from a country of soft days, soft rain, soft light, where the morning quietly clears its throat. Australia's not like that – it's a full roar into the day and how she loves the exuberance of that. Through wide windows the garden greenery tosses in the sea breeze like the heads of wild ponies and nature presses close, she can feel the great thumb of it. She is as calm as an eiderdown, here, within it, an eiderdown lying snugly, quietly, in readiness for its bed. Connie sleeps deeply here, her nights unbroken, for her man strong beside her is like a cool trickle of water upon her soul and it is all bringing her into stillness, to rest, for the first time in her life; she is content, she is content. As she steps into a new life unbound, optimistic, freed, by the truth; as if a great corset has been unloosed.

The author acknowledges with gratitude the words of Virginia Woolf, which provide each chapter with its opening quotation.

P.S.

About the author

About the book

Insights,
Interviews
& More . . .

Read on

Meet Nikki Gemmell

Kathy Luu

NIKKI GEMMELL is the author of several novels, including *Shiver*, *Alice Springs*, *The Book of Rapture*, and the international bestsellers *The Bride Stripped Bare* and *With My Body*. She lives in Sydney, Australia, with her family.

The author of the daringly revealing novel *I Take You* reveals her own loves and fears.

What is your idea of perfect happiness?

Being immersed within my family, somewhere wild by the sea, having just completed a novel I'm satisfied with.

What is your greatest fear?

That my children will be hurt.

Which living person do you most admire?

My husband, for putting up with me.

What objects do you always carry with you?

A notebook, an old Waterman pen, and a lipstick.

What single thing would improve the quality of your life?

More sleep.

What is the most important lesson life has taught you?

Don't let people fool you into giving up; have the courage to follow your heart and do what you really want to do.

Which writer has had the greatest influence on your work?

Michael Ondaatje.

Do you have a favorite children's book?

To Kill a Mockingbird by Harper Lee.

Where is your favorite café/restaurant?

Anywhere that lets me write. At the moment it's Starbucks, because I can work for several hours on just a chai tea and a muffin. I'm sure they loathe customers like me. ▶

3

Meet Nikki Gemmell *(continued)*

Where do you go for inspiration?

Anywhere that's quiet, where I can be alone.

Do you have any pet peeves?

People who are heart sinkers (as opposed to heart lifters): small, ugly-spirited people who want to drag others down.

Which book do you wish you had written?

Jane Eyre. 〜

Try a Little Tenderness

After Fifty Shades of Grey, *how can
a novelist refresh the language of love?
Author Nikki Gemmell decided to update
D. H. Lawrence's* Lady Chatterley's Lover.

HOW EVEN TO BEGIN to take on that
depth charge of a novel, *Lady Chatterley's
Lover*; especially now, in this post–*Fifty
Shades of Grey* world? How to freight
the writing of sex with freshness and
renewal and audacity—with surprise?
Aren't we meant to have seen it all by
now, done it all, thought it all? How
to update the novel's setting from
the forbidding environs of
Nottinghamshire's Wragby Hall,
with its necklace of grubby coal mines
encroaching so dynamically upon it?

D. H. Lawrence despaired that his
world of 1920s England was being
leached of all tenderness. *Tenderness*
was, in fact, the original title of his novel,
and the pursuit of that most gentle and
generous of words is at its core. Lady
Chatterley (Connie) explains to her
gamekeeper lover, Mellors, what's so
extraordinary about him:

> "Shall I tell you what you have that
> other men don't have, and that will
> make the future?"
> "Tell me then," he replied.
> "It's the courage of your own
> tenderness, that's what it is."

Her husband, Clifford, is devoid of it.
Nothing in his statically interior world ▶

of men-who-talk, of philosophizing and writing and books, is instinctive, warm, spontaneous; nothing is deeply felt.

Lawrence's novel is about two people awakening to a new way of living through mutual tenderness, in an exterior world that's uncracking after the long winter hibernation. It's about two people uncurling from previous sexual experiences that have deadened them. There's the shock in the novel of a man who loves women: loves their bodies, cherishes them, is not afraid of them.

Men like that are still hard to find and, when we do, don't we women know it. Lawrence champions a way of being that's instinctive, loving, unafraid—and deeply attuned to nature. Men of that ilk are so rare, still. These issues are just as relevant today and I galloped with the updating, using Lawrence's sincerity as my tuning fork. It's a genuineness that's compelling even now, eighty-five years later. He didn't set out to shock, but merely to be deeply honest.

With my novel *I Take You* the truth, in all is rawness and audacity, is where I began, even if it pushed me into areas that required a lot of courage to name. A scribbled mantra of Milan Kundera's was above the writing desk: "In anguish I imagine a time when art shall cease to seek out the never-said." Another text of brazen eroticism, *The Story of O*, informed the narrative. My book begins with a scenario not dissimilar to poor, deluded O's, but my protagonist's

66 I galloped with the updating, using Lawrence's sincerity as my tuning fork. 99

journey is about climbing away from that world. That had to be the arc of the story. My Connie finds a connection sanctified by tenderness, and is repaired by it.

In this *Fifty Shades* era we're flooded, of course, with a brazen new openness, but is there any emphasis on tenderness? Everyone's seemingly doing it—in increasingly bold ways. Where does it all go from here? Experimentation increasingly permeates the public sphere; the Homebase kink invades suburban bedrooms, and there's raw talk at school gates. The voracious devouring of erotic texts feels revolutionary in terms of women's reading; the dawn of a new age of . . . what?

Could it be that this new decadence represents a tipping-point of some sort? What follows? A flinch into extreme conservatism; a vast reining back? Or a return to a more natural way, with how our bodies look and what we do with them.

That was what interested me in *I Take You*: refinding a more animal, instinctive, earthy way. In *Lady Chatterley's Lover*, the first seduction scene between Connie and Mellors, deep in the woods, is almost hypnotically silent; everything is deeply felt. By the end of the episode, Connie is cracked open, as is Mellors ("the man lay in a mysterious stillness"). Two people have been brought alive through transcendent, utterly natural, deeply tender sex. Don't we all dream of that? ▶

> " My Connie finds a connection sanctified by tenderness, and is repaired by it. "

Try a Little Tenderness *(continued)*

So, to the setting. Who truly inspires wonder and envy and visceral hatred now? Whose secure, pampered, blinkered little world would we like to see called into question? Not so much the upper classes, which seem fractured, crumbling, messy, failing; a product of their own lack of steely, thrusting, twenty-first-century ruthlessness. But then there are the bankers . . .

Until recently, I lived in London's Notting Hill. Raised three kids in it. Had an illegal key to one of its ravishingly beautiful communal gardens, thanks to a succession of good-hearted and better-off American friends who could never get their heads around the willfully antidemocratic nature of the setup: all that caged-off green, so outrageously unfair! I had often toyed with setting a modern *Lady Chatterley* in one of those enchantingly verdant expanses, within the banker world that inspired such envy and loathing among the wider community.

I was fascinated by the endless basement extensions with their screening rooms and nanny's quarters; the four cars, one just for the motorway; the frenzied push to get their children into the best schools; the Guy Fawkes effigies at the communal-garden bonfires wearing Burberry and Barbour; the masculine brusqueness and one-upmanship. Oh yes, my Clifford would be a hedge-fund manager. An American. Dwelling in his leonine way within this

66 Oh yes, my Clifford would be a hedge-fund manager. 99

shockingly unequal world, careering toward the tinderbox of the London riots of summer 2011. In a borough ring-fenced by new worlds, where white Brits are a minority. Lawrence's Mellors was fascinated by the social inequality he saw all around him; I'm a coal miner's daughter from a country a little more meritocratic than this one, and I am also.

So, to the man at the heart of the tale. The male lover. Make him the keeper of one of those exclusive patches of green, its gardener. Oh, they'd watch them, the manicured wives of Notting Hill, sitting on their lovely rolling lawns with their toddlers in Bonpoint and the hovering Filipina nannies. Who better to represent the disgruntled male of the moment? The uneducated, white, working-class British male; the man one assumes would be driving his white van. Who doesn't know how to pronounce words like Cadogan and Cholmondeley. Who's a keen observer of the world around him. Who's utterly surprising as a lover. Step forward, my modern-day Mel.

Connie, the devoted banker's wife, stumbles across him in her communal garden. Finds her voice, strength, audaciousness; her erotic individuality. The vivid core of who she is. The discovery of a female sexual voice, a generation or two earlier than Lawrence, was seen as deeply destructive and unsustainable—just look at Hardy's *Tess of the D'Urbervilles*, Flaubert's ▶

Madame Bovary, Strindberg's *Miss Julie*.
But the discovery of that potency is
something women are just as fascinated
by today; often we don't find our sexual
voice until our thirties, forties. Still.

Connie's journey is one of
empowerment, be that emotional,
psychological, or sexual. And what's
almost as shocking as the erotic honesty
in *Lady Chatterley's Lover* is Connie's
evolving attitude to class and wealth.
Eventually, she longs to reject it all.
For love, for warmth; for the chance
to live fully, richly, simply, sensuously.
Somewhere closer to the earth. Again,
that magnificent relinquishing is relevant
today—it's explored in *I Take You*.

Lady Chatterley's Lover remains
shocking. There are passages, still, that
tug at the belly and quicken the breath.
Why? Their fearless honesty. Luminosity
doesn't kick in until a third of the way
through, though. As Samuel Beckett said
of another Lawrence work, the novella
St. Mawr: "lovely things as usual and
plenty of rubbish."

There was a lot of rubbish to be
discarded as the book was updated.
But I appreciate novels that may be
messy and deeply flawed, yes, yet are
alive, vivid, sparky; books that have
an explosive force about them. *Lady
Chatterley's Lover* does, still, and I hope
my own *I Take You* has something of
that too.

The written word has to compete with
so much else now, to renew itself. Why
not with the shock of the truth? *Lady*

> The written word has to compete with so much else now, to renew itself. Why not with the shock of truth?

Chatterley's Lover still has the power to stun. It's raw and confronting and makes your stomach churn and has you examining your life and your relationships afresh. All power to books that get under your skin. ∾

This essay appeared in the June 1, 2013 edition of The Independent's Radar *magazine.*

Have You Read?
More by Nikki Gemmell

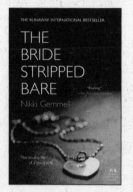

THE BRIDE STRIPPED BARE

A woman disappears, leaving behind an incendiary diary chronicling a journey of sexual awakening. To all who knew her, she was the good wife: happy, devoted, content. But the diary reveals a secret self, one who has discovered that her new marriage contains mysteries of its own.

"Titillating . . . like an artful striptease, *The Bride Stripped Bare* ensnares us with its rawness." —*San Francisco Chronicle*, a Best Book of the Year

"[*The Bride Stripped Bare*] affects a dreamy mood and a poetic brand of erotica." —*New York Times*

A wife, and a mother of three, has everything a woman should want, and yet she has gone numb inside. Only one person, a man from her past, has ever come close to touching the core of her being. In desperation she returns to the memory of this love affair, yet in exploring this transformative relationship, she must be prepared to confront the hidden truths of her heart.

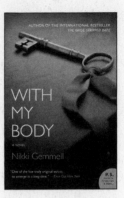

"[Gemmell takes] our Everywoman on a journey from alienated wifehood, back to the past and reimmersion in bodily bliss, then round again to greater self-knowledge and the romance of reborn domesticity. . . . It zips along, providing sexual and romantic thrills."

—*The Guardian*

"Compellingly written. . . . beautiful prose. [Gemmell's] gift for storytelling makes this a rewarding read."

—*Publishers Weekly*

Have You Read? *(continued)*

THE BOOK OF RAPTURE

Three children wake up in a basement room. They have been drugged and taken from their beds in the middle of the night. Where are their parents? Whom can they trust? The family has been betrayed to the government, and Salt Cottage, their home on a cliff top above the ocean, is no longer safe. Their mother's scientific work has put them all in danger. She must put her faith in an old family friend—and in her children's own resilience and courage.

"Haunting, thought-provoking, and beautifully written."   —*Marie Claire*

"[Gemmell's] writing is powerful and heartrending as she delves into the working of human relationships, love, and family."
  —*Courier-Mail* (Queensland, Australia)

LOVESONG

The heartbreaking story of Lillie
Bird, a woman from a locked religious
community who finds freedom at last
in a strange new world, England, but is
accused of murder.

"Gemmell evokes place superbly . . .
while Lillie, clever, confused, and
vulnerable, is real and touching."
—*Sunday Times* (London)

"A lovely, lyrical creation that has melody
and melancholy aching through its
sentences . . . bewitchingly good."
—*Elle*, Book of the Month

ALICE SPRINGS

Snip Freeman lost her father long ago.
Accompanied by her lover, Dave, she
embarks on a journey into the vast
and fierce landscape of the Australian
interior to find her father and unravel
the terrifying silence of her childhood.

"*Alice Springs* is like a female version of
Kerouac's *On the Road*." —*Cosmopolitan*

"Leaks deep into the imagination . . .
haunts one long after the book ends."
—*The Times* (London)

Have You Read? *(continued)*

SHIVER

A young woman, Fin, fulfills her ambition to visit Antarctica, the last great wilderness on earth. Here she integrates with the local community, learning to respect their customs and way of life. But she breaks the strictest taboo of all when she falls in love.

"Gemmell writes brilliantly."
—*Sunday Times* (London)

"Her inimitable, urgent, and demanding style makes her books impossible to put down or forget."
—*Le Figaro Madame* (France)

Don't miss the next book by your favorite author. Sign up now for AuthorTracker by visiting www.AuthorTracker.com.